"When I thought you were dead, it was as though someone had turned a light out inside of me," Dan said quietly, his voice echoing slightly.

"How long did that feeling last—a day?" Cassa asked, cursing herself for not socking Dan in the jaw right then.

"I needed you, Cassa. I always have . . . from the first moment I realized that the sweet little girl I knew had grown into a very lovely young lady, and that I had to marry her."

"Bull," Cassa squawked as she tried to ignore the hand caressing her body. "If you needed me so much—"

"I needed you then. I need you now," Dan interrupted roughly.

Ann Cristy *was born and raised in Rochester, New York, where she still lives with her husband and, off and on, her four grown children. She's an avid skier, swimmer, and weight lifter, and does volunteer work with the handicapped. For her, writing is a way of life.*

Dear Reader:

Spring is here—and so are more TO HAVE AND TO HOLD romances! We began publishing the line just eight months ago, and already we've developed a dedicated and growing following, women (and even some men!) who love TO HAVE AND TO HOLD and buy all three books each month.

TO HAVE AND TO HOLD is the one romance line that's truly different. No other line presents the joys and challenges of married love. And TO HAVE AND TO HOLD offers the variety you crave—from love stories that tug at your heartstrings to those that tickle your funny bone. At the same time, you can trust all TO HAVE AND TO HOLD books to provide you with thoroughly satisfying romantic entertainment.

Your letters continue to pour in—and they're inspiring as well as helpful. All of you share our enthusiasm for the concept behind TO HAVE AND TO HOLD. Many of you also praise individual books and authors. From your letters, it's clear we've convinced you that, in TO HAVE AND TO HOLD, stories of marriage are as exciting and romantic as those of courtship. We're pleased and delighted with your response!

Warm wishes for a beautiful spring,

Ellen Edwards

Ellen Edwards
TO HAVE AND TO HOLD
The Berkley Publishing Group
200 Madison Avenue
New York, N.Y. 10016

HOMECOMING

ANN
CRISTY

A™
SECOND CHANCE AT LOVE
BOOK

Other books by ***Ann Cristy***

Second Chance at Love
FROM THE TORRID PAST #49
TORN ASUNDER #60
ENTHRALLED #103
NO GENTLE POSSESSION #166

To Have and to Hold
TREAD SOFTLY #3

HOMECOMING

First edition published May 1984

First printing

Printed in the United States of America

To Have and to Hold books are published by
The Berkley Publishing Group
200 Madison Avenue, New York, NY 10016

To my uncle, Gilbert Kroubalkian, a man of sublime courage, and to his daughter, Diane, my cousin, who died too young, I dedicate this book.

And to Leslie Kazanjian and others like her who epitomize the charm and class of the Armenians I've known, I also dedicate this book.

I am grateful that you walked through my life.

HOMECOMING

1

SHE WAS FREE! Free! Orly Airport and the American embassy man were behind her now. Ahead was Kennedy Airport in New York, then Rochester. She, Cassa Welles, U.S. citizen, wife of Dan Welles, was going home.

For the last nine months she had been held prisoner in Suwanon, a small sheikhdom situated in the strife-torn area between Lebanon and Syria.

Cassa had gone to the Middle East to purchase some rare Kerman rugs that had been smuggled out of Iran. At an auction of oriental carpets in the Suwanese marketplace she'd struck up a friendly conversation with a man from the French consulate, Marcel Cyr. Discovering that they shared a love of rugs and Middle Eastern culture, she had gladly accepted his invitation to attend a dinner at the consulate that evening. She'd had no idea then how profoundly her life would be changed by that simple act...

As she prepared for that evening dinner, she'd given special care to her appearance, excited by the thought of meeting such interesting and important people. She feared she might be dreaming: it was too good to be true. And even now she could easily recall the dreamlike feeling she'd experienced upon entering the beautiful white building that housed the French consulate. She'd been stunned by the glittering opulence inside.

In the formal dining room she'd been seated next to Marie Dugault, the friend of an embassy official. Cassa and the Frenchwoman had hit it off right away, and they'd chatted pleasantly as course followed course. But then, with no warning at all, Cassa's splendid dream had suddenly become a nightmare.

It was here that Cassa's memories became blurred; she had only a vague recollection of a deafening noise, blinding light... and then nothing. She'd pieced together the sequence of events much later... when time had stretched long and empty ahead of her, and her thoughts had returned again and again to those terrifying moments.

At first Cassa hadn't even realized that the consulate was being bombed. Chaos and destruction had erupted all around her, yet she'd been too stunned to move. Then, without thinking, she'd grabbed Marie's hand and pulled her to a sheltered niche under a stairway. An instant later the stairs had collapsed, burying the two women under a crushing weight. When Cassa regained consciousness, bruised and sore with a deep cut across her upper body, she'd discovered that her purse and passport were gone and that she and the French nationals were being held incommunicado by the group of radical Suwanese that had bombed the consulate. Marie Dugault was dead.

Even now, as the plane sped toward New York, Cassa's skin grew damp with perspiration at the remembered shock of finding herself held prisoner. Thank God her friend from the marketplace, Marcel Cyr, had also survived the bombing. He'd urged her not to tell their captors that she was an American with no passport, explaining she'd be much better off if the Suwanese thought she was Marie Dugault.

"As a Frenchwoman, you will be protected as much as possible by my country, cherie," he had said, embracing her. "My countrymen will negotiate for our freedom, and then later you can reveal your true identity. You will be able to get another passport in Paris."

"But my husband will think I'm dead," Cassa had protested.

"That, cherie, is the least of our worries," Marcel Cyr had replied with hardheaded practicality, an attitude that helped her many times in the difficult months that had followed. And now . . . now she was going home.

She had called her brother Len, a lawyer from the American embassy in Paris because Marcel had suggested it would be wise to seek legal advice. She had wanted to call her husband—her dear, beloved Dan—but there hadn't been time before the plane took off, and she had been so anxious to get home . . .

"I'm going home," she whispered, her breath ragged, her throat tight. "I'm free. I'm free."

For nine months she had been held in a house with a tiny walled garden out back, where she had paced the perimeter from dawn until dark, sometimes jogging in place, sometimes dragging her feet, desperately needing to keep moving so as not to go mad. Once a week the Suwanese had allowed her to talk to Marcel Cyr, but even then an armed guard had been present, listening to every word they said.

Cassa glanced casually out of the plane window. The sight of the Statue of Liberty directly below froze her to the seat, and she kept her eyes glued to the somewhat shabby but still proud lady. How ironic that the French should have given you to the United States, and now they are giving me back to my country too, she thought, her throat tight with unshed tears.

Give me your tired, your poor, your huddled masses
yearning to breathe free,
The wretched refuse of your teeming shore,
Send these, the homeless, tempest tossed, to me:
I lift my lamp beside the golden door.

When the plane landed, Cassa was ushered into the VIP lounge by a flight attendant and a uniformed airlines official. She was there only a moment before the door opened, letting in the noise of Kennedy Airport and a tall, lithe man with reddish hair. "Len!"

"Cassa!" He raced to her, arms outstretched, to envelope her in a crushing embrace. "Cassa, it's really you. You're alive!"

"Oh, Len, I'm so happy to be home. I can't believe it's really you."

They pulled slightly apart, and she stared at his well-remembered features, swallowing painfully around the tightness in her throat. He hadn't changed much, though it seemed like a million years since she'd last seen him. His chestnut hair, so unlike her own wavy black tresses, was still straight, though she detected a more generous sprinkling of gray. He had the same gray eyes, so like her own. But there was a weary, even sad look about him. Of course, after nine months in Suwanon, she was sure she must look different to him as well.

"Cassa, wc thought you were dead," Len rasped, pulling her close again. His laugh quavered as he leaned back slightly to draw a finger down her cheek.

"Am I the only one who knows you're alive?" She nodded, and he shook his head. "Lord, you're so thin. You're like a little lost soul. Your eyes are too large for your face, and your bones look so fragile." He stroked her skin, teary-eyed, the words seeming to come without his volition. "Whatever happened to those hips you wanted to diet away?" His grin wobbled and her heart went out to him.

"I managed to get rid of the extra padding." Cassa couldn't seem to clear her own voice of its huskiness as she struggled to control her overwhelming emotions. "I did quite a bit of jogging in the small space I was allotted."

The smile left his face. "Oh Lord, Cassa. You must have been so frightened." He hugged her again.

"I was," she whispered into his shoulder. "But I'm free now. Free. You don't know what that means to me." She pressed against him. "It's so good to see you, brother mine. There were moments when I didn't think I ever would again."

They stood holding one another, unspoken questions heavy between them. But they couldn't ask them yet.

"When the Bureau of Consular Affairs called my office and said you wished to speak to me, I almost had a heart attack." Len laughed weakly. "We thought you were dead.

They told us the bodies were so badly mutilated—" He stopped abruptly.

"I know. That's what they said at the embassy in Paris. They found pieces of my passport and other identification, so . . ." Cassa didn't want to talk about it anymore. Only one thing interested her. "How's Dan? Is he all right?"

Len was about to answer when an officious-looking man in a dark suit approached them. Len held out his hand. "You must be Mr. Lawrence of the Bureau of Consular Affairs. We spoke on the phone. I'm Len Davis."

"It's good to meet you. Ordinarily our job is finished once an American national arrives home, but I wanted to say how sorry we are that your sister was detained in Suwanon for such a long time." He shrugged, his smile barely creasing his face. "Of course, if we had known she was there, we would have immediately taken steps to secure her release. As it was, we didn't even know she was alive until the prisoners were exchanged and she was released with the French nationals." His lips were pursed as he turned to Cassa. "Actually, we would not have recommended assuming the Dugault's woman's identity . . . but we realize the danger of being in that area without papers, in effect a stateless person."

"I might have been imprisoned in far worse surroundings if the Suwanese hadn't considered me a valuable hostage," Cassa explained to Len.

Mr. Lawrence inclined his head. "Shall we simply agree that all's well that ends well? Mrs. Welles is a free woman now." He gave a small smile and walked away.

"I'm free, I'm free," Cassa murmured. "I've been saying that all the way across the Atlantic." Free to go home to Dan, to be held by him, loved by him. Free to return to Tijanian's, the oriental rug business they had worked so hard to build into a thriving concern, with stores in Buffalo and Syracuse as well as Rochester. Oh, Dan, I'm coming home to you, Cassa's heart sang.

"You're free." Len kissed her cheek.

Cassa stopped abruptly, her hand to her mouth. "I'm so crazy right now, I forgot to ask you about Maddy. How is she? Did she come with you?" She sensed his hesitation and panic ballooned inside her. "Is something wrong with Maddy? Or is it Dan? Please tell me, is Dan all right?"

"Of course he is." Len guided her toward the door. "Now let's hurry. You told me you wanted to get to Rochester as soon as possible so I booked a flight"—he shot out his left wrist—"that leaves in twenty minutes."

Cassa could hardly suppress her questions, but the urge to get home was paramount. Half running, half walking, she and Len headed toward the gate where their plane was waiting. She tried to ignore the anxiety that made her cling to her brother as they fought their way through the noisy, pressing crowds.

It was a relief to board the comparatively quiet plane that would take them to Rochester, the city of her birth, the place where she had gone to school and met her beloved husband. She was going home.

She glanced at her brother as he buckled his seat belt, drawing strength from his presence. She smiled as he began flirting with the pretty flight attendant. Len had always been popular with the ladies—until he'd married Maddy, that is. Cassa plucked at his sleeve, reclaiming his attention. "Len, tell me what's happened. You know I can always sense it when you have a problem."

Len took a deep breath before turning to her. "Maddy and I have split," he said abruptly. "I understand she's going to marry Jack Dexter after our divorce is final."

"Jack Dexter, the dentist you used to golf with at the club?"

Len nodded.

"But you and Maddy love each other! You always have."

Cassa felt as though one corner of the foundation holding up her life had been pulled out from under her. Len and Maddy had been a stabilizing influence ever since she and Len had lost their parents in an automobile accident two years after Cassa'd married Dan. She and Maddy were more like real sisters than in-laws.

"Things change, Cass," Len began, then shook his head, rubbing a hand across his forehead. "Dammit, Cassa, I don't know what happened. She thought . . ." He ground his teeth. "Let's not discuss it now. We have other things to talk about before the plane lands," he added with a smile.

Sensing his wariness, Cassa didn't smile back. "What else is wrong? Is it about Dan?"

"Yes." He took hold of her hand and stroked it soothingly. "I haven't seen much of him since shortly after we got the news of your death."

"Which was greatly exaggerated," Cassa quipped dryly.

"Greatly," Len agreed, his smile fleeting. "Dan seemed to retreat into himself. He refused all my invitations, and when I saw Maddy, she said the same. He didn't golf anymore. No one saw him on the handball courts at the Y. He began jogging on his own, keeping to himself, working all hours of the day and night."

The stewardess returned, and Cassa listened with half an ear as her brother bantered with the woman. Cassa's thoughts were confused and fragmented. Without thinking, she raised a hand to her hair, loving the satin feel of the freshly washed strands. Being allowed only one shampoo and one shower per week had been just one of the many deprivations she'd suffered these last nine months. *I'm free!* The thought echoed in her mind again and again. *I'm going home and I'm free!*

"Your hair is beautiful, sister mine," Len said softly in her ear. "I don't remember it ever being so long, or so wavy. You look like a sleek panther with your long legs, swanlike neck, and silvery eyes."

"Such flattery from a brother," Cassa laughed, but her heart was heavy. Len was clearly reluctant to say more about Dan.

"Let me finish," Len chided her. "You have the skin of an English schoolgirl."

"Good finish." Cassa tried to smile.

The flight attendant brought the drinks Len had ordered.

Cassa glanced out the window at the fleecy clouds that seemed to be cushioning the plane. What was Len hiding from her? She swallowed, her mouth dry. Whatever it was, she would face it somehow. Now that she was home she felt she could face anything.

Suddenly the mental and physical strain of the previous forty-eight hours caught up with her. Her heavy eyelids fluttered and then closed. At once in her mind's eye she saw the laughing young woman who had married Daniel Casemore Welles eight years ago. The vision took her even further back in time to the night she'd first met Dan. A university chum of Len's, Dan had come to dinner one evening when Cassa was fifteen and he was twenty-one. Dan had explained that he'd taken a year off from school in order to earn enough money to continue. His parents lived in the northern California town of Surrey, where he had been raised.

Cassa had stared and stared at Dan all through dinner, blushing each time he glanced her way and smiled.

She had tried hard to join the conversation after dinner, but Len, Dan, and her father had watched a hockey game on television. Cassa, who knew very little about the game, sat stiff and bored through all two and a half hours of it, hoping to convince Dan that they shared a vital interest.

From then on, Dan had been a frequent guest of the Davises, joining them for weekends and holidays.

After graduation Len went into the insurance business with Cassa's father and became engaged to the pretty and petite Madeleine Louise Tellier, from Montreal, who had just graduated from the Rochester Institute of Technology, where she'd majored in design. Maddy opened a small shop in downtown Rochester with her friend from French Canada, Girardot LeBlanc, who had also attended RIT.

In the meantime, Dan left the area to attend the Wharton School of Business in Pennsylvania. He returned two years later to work for a large conglomerate, and soon began to see Cassa in a very different way—as a woman, not a kid sister. They married as soon as Dan agreed she was old enough: she was nineteen; he was twenty-five. Two years later she graduated from RIT with a degree in business. That same year her parents were killed in a freak automobile accident. Cassa felt she reached her maturity in the painful months that followed, when Dan's comfort and support sustained her.

Shortly after the wedding Cassa's uncle, Aram Tijanian, owner of Tijanian's Oriental Rugs, Inc., urged Dan to leave his well-paying job and learn the oriental rug trade. For Dan the offer represented a business challenge plus a chance to gain the independence he'd always wanted, and he accepted gladly.

Dan quickly became a valued member of the company, using all his considerable energies and talents to make it grow. By the time Uncle Aram died a short six months later, Dan had opened stores in both Syracuse and Buffalo.

The shock of losing three of the closest people in her life almost tore Cassa apart. More and more she turned to Dan, her ever-present bulwark. Shoring her up against the grief that threatened to overwhelm her, he made every effort to bring joy and laughter back into her life.

They joined the country club, they partied, they traveled to Colorado to ski. They decided to put off having a family until they were financially secure and had had a chance to enjoy life together, just the two of them. They made adventurous journeys to Turkey, for pleasure and to buy rugs. Dan had intended to travel with Cassa to Suwanon, but an emergency had arisen in the Syracuse store, and she'd gone alone . . .

Cassa's eyes flew open. She didn't want to think about Suwanon ever again. She stared out at the cottony clouds, willing herself to think of Rochester: their store, Tijanian's, on East Avenue; the Eastman Theater and Kilbourn Hall, located just around the corner, where the Eastman School of Music held student concerts. Next door to Tijanian's was a music shop with grand pianos in the window. It always delighted Cassa to hear the music through the walls of the store.

She squeezed her eyes shut and recalled Gellert's, where she and Dan sometimes ate breakfast. The restaurant was always crowded before an Eastman concert. She could almost hear the carillon of Christ Church on East Avenue, the sounds of music students practicing their cellos, violins, and flutes.

She sighed and swallowed. *Going home, going home* the airplane engines thrummed. Cassa sighed contentedly.

Len turned to her. "Did you say something? I thought you were asleep."

"I was just dreaming, remembering." She pressed her head against the cushioned seat. "You were telling me something about Dan," she reminded him.

Len nervously licked his bottom lip.

Cassa remembered the characteristic gesture. "What is it? Tell me," she insisted, her stomach tightening into knots.

Len rubbed his forehead wearily. "I only know what I've heard. There are rumors that he's been seeing Carla Warders."

"The lawyer?" Cassa whispered, shocked.

"Yes." Len shifted in his seat. "It was none of my business. You were gone, or so we thought . . ."

"I understand," Cassa said stiffly. But I don't understand, not at all, she cried silently; I was coming back to you, Dan . . . to our life, to freedom, to our home in Cornhill, to the business. How could you choose someone else so fast? How could you replace me with another woman?

"It will be different, now that you're back," Len said, studying her carefully.

"Of course." A false smile widened her mouth. "I . . . I guess I'm still tired. Maybe I'll try to take another nap."

"Sure." Len regarded her with concern and took her hand in his. "Listen to me, Cass. I've known Carla since undergraduate days. She always had a thing for Dan. He always liked her, but it was you he loved. Thinking you were dead . . ."

"I understand." Cassa pressed his hand. But I don't understand, she thought. You should have waited for me, Dan. I need you.

A voice deep inside her, the voice that sustained her many times through loneliness and fear in Suwanon, answered: Stop being a fool, Cassa. You survived imprisonment. You'll survive this. "I won't leave the business," she muttered aloud. "Or the house—Uncle Aram's legacy to me."

"What did you say?" Len looked at her again.

"Nothing." Cassa closed her eyes and tried to banish the images of Dan that danced before her eyes.

The plane landed at Monroe County Airport. Since neither Cassa nor Len had any luggage—Cassa's few possessions easily fit into her large, new handbag—they went directly to Len's car.

As they headed into town, Cassa avidly gazed at the familiar sights along the way.

"Look the same?" Len asked. They were speeding down the expressway toward the older restored section of Rochester, which some called the Third Ward and others, including Cassa and Dan, called Cornhill, the name the early settlers had given the area. The modern-day inhabitants who had restored the dilapidated buildings into comfortable brick and wood dwellings, were justifiably proud of their accomplishment.

"Listen to me, Cass," Len said seriously. "The press will want to know a few things, but if you like, I'll handle them for you."

"Oh please, Len, I don't want to be interviewed. I'll give you a statement and you do it."

He squeezed her knee. "No problem."

As they left the highway at the Plymouth Avenue exit, Cassa felt perspiration bead her upper lip. She and Len drove in tense silence.

"Cassa, maybe we should have called Dan from the airport," Len said anxiously. "Maybe you should come with me to my apartment. We can get in touch with Dan from there."

"No," Cassa said softly. "I want to go home. I need a change of clothes. I've worn hand-me-downs for too long." She felt the smile slipping off her face, and she struggled to hold back her growing fear. "I'm free," she whispered again. "I want to take a shower in my own bathroom, dress in something that doesn't hang on me like a bag."

"I'm afraid your old clothes will hang on you anyway, Cass," Len reminded her gently. "You must be sizes smaller than you were." He grinned, but his gray eyes glistened with concern.

"Yes, I suppose I am. It doesn't matter. It will be heaven to wear something that belongs to me." Her voice almost cracked, and she bit her lower lip.

Len nodded. "Home it is, lady."

"Thank you."

As they wove down the narrow streets of Cornhill, a tense silence filled the car like the calm before a storm.

Cassa was almost sure Len could hear the slow thunder of her heart.

When they drew up before the corner house on Atkinson Street that her Armenian uncle Aram had left her, Cassa sighed deeply.

Len stopped the car and turned to her, his right arm along the back of the seat. "It will take a while for me to get used to you with long hair, but I do like it. Mother always kept your hair cropped short."

"If she hadn't, I would have cut it myself. I was involved in too many sports to want to fuss with it."

Len leaned over and kissed her cheek. "Now it looks like a midnight waterfall, swept back from your face like that. You're so lovely, Cass." He smiled, but his eyes were grave, as though he too were nervous.

Cassa knew her brother was trying to prepare himself as well as her for what they might have to face inside. Glancing around her, she suddenly noticed the many cars lining the opposite side of the narrow street and the lights shining in the windows of number 14. "It looks like Dan is entertaining," she said uncertainly.

Len followed her gaze. "I still think it would be better if we went to my apartment and called him from there."

"No," Cassa said firmly. "This is my home." Her voice softened. "Sorry, but I think I'd better deal with this now."

Len nodded and got out of the car. Before he could go around to Cassa's door, she was out on the sidewalk, and looking up at the mellow, pinkish brick building with the black shutters and matching double front doors. A wrought-iron street lamp cast a pale glow on the house, making the brass knockers on each door gleam.

For a brief moment time seemed to stand still, and Cassa's life with Dan flashed before her eyes. She saw the eager young woman she had been on her wedding day, just nineteen and with two years of college still to go. Their honeymoon in the Far East had been heaven on earth. They had laughed, made love, revealed their innermost selves to each other, made wonderful plans for their future. It was then that Cassa had first suggested that Dan talk to her Uncle Aram about going into business with him.

"Darling," Dan had crooned as they lay on their private beach, the warm water lapping at their feet, "I already have a good job. It's interesting." His eyes had a faraway look as he had peeled her bikini top from her body.

"I know." She had run her fingers down his cheek. "But Uncle Aram will be giving the business to me one day, and it would be nice if we could run it together . . . wouldn't it?"

"Doing anything together with you would be more than nice, angel." Dan had kissed her body from ear to ankle and back again.

That had been the first of many such discussions they'd had over the years; until finally, shortly before Uncle Aram's death, Dan had decided to leave his large company and join Tijanian's. The change proved to be not only a good business move but a great comfort to Cassa when she lost her beloved uncle.

Joining the country club had seemed a matter of course. They'd hardly discussed doing so. Being athletic, Cassa enjoyed playing golf as well as getting together with the new friends they made. Although she sometimes found all the socializing a bit wearing, especially after her long, hard hours at the store, Cassa had been delighted with her life as Dan's wife. Dan couldn't have been happier. He was thriving at the store and fully enjoying the people at the club. And Cassa had to admit that when Dan was happy, she was happy. It was really very simple.

"Hey, little sister, why are you staring at the front door? Daydreaming?" Len asked softly.

Cassa blinked, then turned to him. "That's impossible. It's nighttime. Daydreaming is for the day." Feeling as though her face would crumble if she smiled, she stared at the house that held so many wonderful memories, not only of her marriage, but also of her childhood, when she'd come here to stay with her aunt and uncle. "This has always been such a happy house, Len," she said.

"Yes." He put his arm around her shoulders. "It was a fun place to visit when we were children. We were lucky to have parents and an aunt and uncle who loved us so much."

Together they walked up the front steps. As Len moved

to lift one of the brass door knockers, Cassa stayed his hand.

"Have you forgotten where Uncle Aram used to hide the key?"

For a moment Len looked puzzled, and then he smiled. "You mean you still keep a key there?"

"We always kept one here..." Cassa pushed aside a loose brick near the door, revealing a small hollowed-out space, and removed a brass key. She unlocked the door and pushed it inward. Laughter and the clinking of glasses—the sounds of a party well under way—assaulted her ears.

2

DAN SHOULDN'T BE having a party when she wasn't there with him. Unreasoning emotion replaced logic as Cassa and Len moved through the doorway into a spacious foyer, now empty, tiled in black and white marble. A graceful floating stairway dominated the area.

Double doors leading to the living room stood open, and Cassa vaguely recognized several of the laughing people holding their champagne glasses high. For a moment she felt as though she and Len were invisible, silent witnesses to a macabre *bal masqué*. Why were all these people in her house? She recognized Will Bishop, a wine importer, who was both a friend and business associate. She saw people she knew from the club—women she had golfed with, men who'd played tennis with Dan.

As if in slow motion she watched Carla Warders circulate among the guests, playing the role of hostess. Cassa seethed with resentment. Even without Len's sharp intake of breath, she would have noticed her sister-in-law—her soon to be *ex*–sister-in-law. Maddy hadn't changed; she was still tiny and beautifully groomed, her well-designed clothes a perfect advertisement for her successful dress shop.

Cassa wanted to move forward and greet people, but her shoes seemed nailed to the floor. Her throat had gone dry, and she was unable to utter a sound. Suddenly Carla raised her hands for quiet and gestured toward a tall, gaunt man whom Cassa recognized as Dave Winters, another acquaintance from the club.

"Wait. Wait everyone," Carla called from the center of the milling throng. "Dave wants to make our announcement for us." She flapped her hands again and peered over people's heads to a corner of the room Cassa couldn't see. "Darling, come over here with me."

The guests parted like the Red Sea, and Daniel Welles walked past them into Cassa's view. Time seemed to stand still as all of her senses focused on her husband. He was much thinner than before, and his face—so familiar yet so changed—appeared graven with weariness, despite his ironic smile. Had his mouth always been that hard? When had his blue eyes lost their tender gaze? Had his hair been so gray at the temples when she left? He still looked like a tall, lean football player, but he'd lost the glow of health and strength that had made him so attractive.

"Darling..." Carla's bell-like tones rose over the crowd's chatter. "Isn't it sweet that Dave wants to announce our engagement for us?" she cooed. "I know you didn't want any formal announcement, or even a party, but don't you think this is cute?"

Dan's half-smile disappeared altogether, and his mouth firmed into a thin line. "Very cute." His voice was flat, expressionless.

Carla laughed. Most of the others followed suit.

Without thinking Cassa moved forward, making her way through the shifting crowd as Dave Winters urged, "Come on, everyone refill your champagne glasses. I'd like to make a toast."

Step by step she moved forward into the room, Len at her heels. Cassa felt as if she were walking in slow motion. The crowd seemed to expand and multiply. Gradually a few people became aware of her presence. Their smiles abruptly disappeared, replaced by expressions of stunned disbelief.

Stifled gasps and startled exclamations punctuated the social chatter as she continued her measured walk. Tense silence followed in her wake.

Dan, Carla, and the people closest to them took no notice of Cassa's approach until she spoke. "I think"—she coughed to clear her throat and tried again—"I think that any engagement announcement is highly premature."

One by one the last voices faded into silence. Cassa felt rather than saw Dan turn toward her. She never took her eyes off Carla. "Married men do not announce"—again her voice faltered as shock and anger warred within her—"their plans to marry other women. In fact, this entire gathering strikes me as being highly inappropriate."

Somehow she managed to turn her eyes to the ashen-faced man coming toward her.

"Cassa?" Dan asked hoarsely. "Cassa? You're alive? How—?" His breath seemed to be torn from his throat as his arms rose to embrace her, then fell to his sides when she stepped backward.

"Yes, I'm alive. I'm free." Her voice seemed to come from far away as she became acutely aware of the stunned faces surrounding her. "I'm happy to see . . . most of you." She tried to smile as everyone began talking at once, crowding around her, firing questions, overwhelming her. Vaguely she heard Len tell everyone to back off, they would learn the whole story in time. But most of Cassa's attention focused on Dan, who seemed frozen to the spot, his eyes riveted on her, his expression utterly unreadable.

"Darling!" Maddy pushed her way to Cassa's side, tears streaming down her face, her arms reaching out and enveloping her in a comforting embrace. Jack Dexter was directly behind Maddy, his face concerned. "How . . . what happened?"

As Cassa hugged her diminutive sister-in-law, she felt Maddy's body stiffen suddenly and knew she'd seen Len. She pulled back from Maddy, holding both her hands. "Len met me at Kennedy Airport. I called him from Paris, where I was taken after my release. All this time I've been held prisoner as a French national, going by the name of Marie Dugault. My own papers and identification were destroyed, the real Marie Dugault was killed in the fire bombing of the consulate, and—" Cassa stopped abruptly. There was too much to explain.

"You didn't think to call me?" Dan croaked. He stood so close that his body almost touched hers.

"Darling," Carla interjected. "I'm sure Cassa knew what she was doing." She slipped her hand through his arm. "We're both so glad you're safe, Cassa," she murmured.

"Are you?" Cassa looked pointedly at the hand clutching Dan's arm, then slid her eyes up his body to his face. His pale complexion had turned a dull red. All at once her pain and fear, her helplessness and shock came together with explosive force, building and building inside her. He'd betrayed her!

"I was told you were dead," Dan muttered. "They said you'd been burned beyond recognition, that it was fortunate they were able to find the remains of your passport." His words faded as he studied her. "You're very thin," he said tightly. "Have you been ill?"

"I've been held prisoner. The food was not exactly bountiful," she shot back at him, her pain erupting in angry words. She could kill him, maim him, for wanting to marry another woman.

"I didn't know." Dan's voice sounded hollow even to his own ears, but inside he was shouting: Cassa, Cassa, how could you have done this to me—put me through hell for no reason? My poor angel, if I had only known you were alive. I died a thousand deaths without you.

He realized he was trembling. Good Lord but he was coming back to life with a vengeance! All the pain he thought he'd buried was rising to the surface in a mighty wave. What were these people doing here? Why were they here when all he wanted was to be alone with his wife?

"I didn't know you were alive," he repeated helplessly.

Anger burst out of Cassa like a volcanic eruption. He hadn't known! She had struggled to survive, to come back to him, to be free . . . and he hadn't even known she was alive! Panic, hostility, fear rose inside her like hot lava under unbearable pressure. She brought back her fist in a short arc. At that moment she could indeed have killed him. "You bastard! What do you know about anything?"

He saw the blow coming, but didn't try to avoid it. He almost welcomed it, rejoicing in any contact with Cassa that would prove she was really here, that she wasn't just the figment of his imagination who had accompanied him through the nightmare of his life for the past nine months.

She struck him so hard that she hurt her hand, but elation filled her when she saw his head snap back and a white mark appear beneath his eye. Immediately the flesh began to swell and discolor.

Carla screamed. Others gasped. Len grabbed Cassa's arm.

"Leave her alone," Dan commanded, one hand moving slowly to his cheek. He hated to see anyone touch her, even her own brother. Darling, you're home, he thought jubilantly. He opened his mouth, his eyes fixed on her.

"No!" The word erupted from her throat. Then she turned and hurried from the room, her long strides taking her out to the foyer and up the floating staircase two steps at a time.

She plunged through the doorway of the master suite, hardly glancing at the cream-colored walls and furnishings, the turquoise accent pillows, the Kerman carpet, the king-sized bed with its coverlet of turquoise and cream in a Chinese design.

She marched down the narrow hallway leading off the bedroom and into a walk-in closet. She'd always used the right side of the closet, but now she stared at the vast empty space, at the bare wooden hangers.

"Where are my clothes?" she said out loud, fear, a familiar emotion, raising goose bumps on her arms. For a brief moment the terror of imprisonment washed over her again—the utter powerlessness, the total lack of any personal possessions.

Whirling, she raced out of the room to the attic doorway. Wrenching it open, she ran up the short flight of stairs and pawed frantically through the garment bags hanging there. Her clothes weren't here either. Panic overwhelming her, she retraced her steps across the upper hall to the stairway and leaned over the bannister. Through a red haze she saw that some of the people were leaving, others were still firing questions at Len. Dan was standing with Carla and Maddy on either side of him, a few feet away from the remaining guests.

"Where are my clothes?" Cassa shouted. She glared at Dan's upraised face.

Before he could answer, Carla stepped in front of him. "But, darling, Cassa, surely you can see how painful it would have been for Dan to keep seeing all your things. I gave them to the Salvation Army." Carla's perfectly made-up face glowed in the rosy light of the chandelier.

"You gave away my clothes?" Cassa was seething. She hated this woman who had dared usurp her place at Dan's side. Pressing her lips together, she leaned down and removed the low-heeled sandal from her right foot. Leaning far out over the balustrade, she flung it straight at Carla. The shoes didn't fit her anyway. "Here's something you forgot." Cassa watched as Dan reached around Carla and deftly caught the shoe.

Carla's face lost all it's color. "Dan, darling, if you hadn't caught it, I would have been struck in the face!" she exclaimed.

Dan ignored her. Staring up at Cassa, seeing the healthy anger on her beloved face, his heart lightened. They hadn't broken her spirit. She was dreadfully thin, and fear shadowed her eyes, but they hadn't broken her. My angel, he cried silently, what did they do to you? A shudder rippled along his tense muscles.

"She always was a good shot," Len observed dryly, glancing from Carla to his sister and chuckling.

"You won't be laughing when I sue you and that paranoid sister of yours," Carla snapped.

"Then stop baiting her," Maddy retorted, her tiny body quivering with unaccustomed anger. "She's been to hell and back, and you're acting as though she just came home from a Caribbean cruise!"

"Now, Maddy," Jack Dexter said soothingly. "Carla was only telling Cassa—"

"She has no right to tell Cassa anything," Maddy interrupted. "When I think of what she must have been through . . ."

Immediately Dan experienced a vivid image of what imprisonment in the Middle East could mean. Bile rose in his throat.

Len looked at Maddy for a moment, and put his arm around her. "You're right, of course." He glanced up at Cassa. "Come on, honey, let me take you to my place. We'll get some clothes for you first thing in the morning."

"No!" Maddy interjected. "She'll come home with me. My clothes will fit you, Cassa, since you've lost so much weight. They might be a little on the short side but—"

"She's staying here." Dan's tone silenced them all. The thought of Cassa leaving to go anywhere was more than he could bear. "After I take Carla home, Maddy, I'll swing past your place and pick up some clothes for Cassa."

"I don't give a damn what anyone does, I'm going to bed," Cassa blurted out. She paused for a moment on the landing, and her tone softened. "Thank you for offering to help, Maddy. I'll come to the shop tomorrow."

"Good. Come early. We'll have breakfast together if you like, then we'll go through the stock to see what we can find. Girardot will want to be there, I'm sure. You can talk to him about any custom-mades you'd like. Good night, Cassa." She paused before adding in a voice tight with sudden tears, "I'm so glad you're home."

Dan had been anticipating a difficult scene with Carla, but he was stunned to find that she expected to go on as though Cassa hadn't returned.

"Look, Carla," Dan said, swerving around a truck that was backing into the avenue as he drove her to her apartment on East Avenue. "Cassa is back and we're still married."

"Darling!" Her laugh tinkled through the car, the sound grating on his nerves. "Surely you've heard of divorce."

"No, Carla. I am not divorcing Cassa." Dan spoke each word clearly, punching the steering wheel for emphasis as he pulled into the parking lot next to Carla's modern apartment building.

"She may wish to divorce you, Dan." Carla walked next to him toward the building. "Would you slow down a bit please? We're not in a race."

"Maddy is waiting up for me," Dan mumbled, walking

with her into the elevator and punching number 5 on the console.

"I'm sure Maddy is with Jack right now, darling. Why not have a drink with me and let them finish... whatever it is they're doing," Carla suggested as she stepped from the elevator and inserted her key in the lock.

Dan felt a sudden distaste for Carla's company. "Good night, Carla. When you see me again, it will be with my wife." He stepped back into the elevator, pressed the button, and watched the doors close without another word.

He arrived at Maddy's house a few minutes later. She opened the door almost as the bell rang.

"Dan. Oh Dan, isn't it wonderful?" She waved him inside and pointed to the suitcase she'd packed for Cassa. "Everything but shoes in here. Tomorrow we'll pick up some clothes at my shop."

"I'll be coming too. I want to make sure she gets enough." Dan's face felt stiff, his smile forced. He had always been close to Maddy, but now he thought that if he tried to talk, express his feelings about Cassa's homecoming, he would fall apart. "I have to go."

"I know." Maddy reached up and kissed his cheek. "Go home, Dan."

Cassa didn't expect to sleep. She was wound up like a spring and uncomfortable in the unfamiliar guest room. She didn't feel at home in her own house anymore.

After undressing, she slid into the cold bed and automatically put a rein on her thoughts—just as she'd done every night in Suwanon. Her imagination took her away to a warm, soft place with no walls, no restrictions, where everyone was free. But Dan's face appeared in her mind's eye almost at once. Though she struggled and fought against it, she felt the delicious warmth of his body as he enclosed her in his arms. Soothed by the thought that she was truly home because Dan was there, she fell into the black well of sleep.

When Dan returned home, panic filled him like a choking cloud. Cassa wasn't in the master suite! Rushing through the rooms of the big house, he finally found her curled into a tight ball in the guest-room bed.

For a moment he considered carrying her to their room, but he was afraid of waking her. Instead, he stripped off his clothes and slid in beside her. No power in the world could have kept him from curving his body around hers and enveloping her like a blanket. He was sure the thudding of his heart against her back would rouse her; but she continued to sleep peacefully and after a few moments he relaxed. Once she wriggled her bottom against him, and his pulse rocketed out of control.

He willed himself to waken early, and, as usual, his built-in alarm clock didn't fail him. He opened his eyes, and for a moment the black, heavy emptiness returned, as it had every morning since he'd first heard the news of Cassa's death. Then he felt her delicate body, still curled against his, shift slightly, and he wanted to weep. His body trembled with remembered joy as he rubbed against her in delight. "I love you, Cassa mine," he whispered before easing out of bed to stand looking down at her, a quiet hunger coursing through his body at the thought of having her again. He left the room silently.

Cassa woke because her back was cold. Squinting against the bright sunlight, she quickly realized where she was. Her prayers had been answered. She was home. Thanking all the gods of all men everywhere, curious and a bit uneasy, she turned over, then sat bolt upright in bed. The pillow next to hers was indented where a head had obviously rested on it.

Clutching the percale sheets, which smelled faintly of the outdoors, Cassa stared at the pillow. She inhaled the fragrant linens, remembering that Mrs. Bills, their housekeeper, always hung them outside on a line strung between two poles.

"Matt the Cat!" she said out loud. "Of course. He must have come in the window and slept with me." Matt the Cat was the steel-willed marmalade tomcat who had adopted Cassa and Dan when they'd first moved into Uncle Aram's house. A veteran stray, he had resisted all their efforts to break him of his nocturnal habits, but perhaps he'd changed during her absence. Maybe he decided to start sleeping in the house at night, Cassa argued with herself, though deep down she was pretty sure it was Dan who'd slept with her . . . that it was his warmth she was missing now.

She shook her head, unwilling to dwell on such thoughts. She was home; that was the important thing. She would deal with everything else one moment at a time.

Yawning and stretching, she swung her legs over the side of the bed, was suddenly aware of how bony they were. "What does it matter, Cassa, my girl?" she quizzed the mirror as she studied her naked form. She might look a bit thin, but she wasn't weak, wasn't sick. She held her hands high in the air. "I'm strong. I'm strong," she repeated, just as she had every morning in Suwanon while jogging around the small enclosed yard.

She padded naked to the bathroom, reveling in her privacy, delighted to be in her own home, in a well-appointed bathroom, with all the soap and hot water she could want. At least Carla hadn't given that to the Salvation Army. "Oooh, this feels so good," she said out loud, sudsing and splashing her body.

"Sybarite." Dan's soft voice penetrated the roar of the shower, and Cassa's eyes flew open. He was standing in the open doorway of the stall.

A glob of foam slipped down her face, and she closed her eyes and yelped, "Get out of here. You've made me get shampoo in my eyes."

"Hold still."

Cassa felt his hand at her waist, pulling her out from under the spray, his other hand going to her face. She flailed at him, crying "Stop! I'll do it myself." She brought her hand up to push him away, but his fingers only tightened around her.

"Stop wriggling," he ordered huskily.

Cassa could feel his eyes on her naked flesh. She wanted to turn away from him, but his gaze was mesmerizing and held her rooted to the spot. Suddenly he gasped, and she stiffened.

"Cassa? What happened to your shoulder?" His hand was gently probing the pink puckered scar that crossed her upper body like a macabre purse strap.

When she felt his mouth on the wound, not even the sting of soap in her eyes could erase the pleasure of his touch. Now she was finally home.

Slowly, unemotionally, she answered his question. "I scrambled under a staircase with another woman when the building blew up. But"—she paused, swallowing—"the stairway collapsed on both of us. That was how the mix-up of papers occurred. We were both carrying our passports in our purses. Pieces of the building were flying around us. Everything caught fire. A piece of wood hit me on the shoulder and knocked me out. By the time I regained consciousness, my shoulder was bandaged and"—she took deep breaths as the painful memories threatened to overwhelm her—"Marie was dead, and they assumed I was she. I didn't try to dissuade them because—"

"Don't," Dan interrupted. "Len told us someone convinced you it would be safer to assume her identity." Dan's hand gently stroked her waist.

"Most of the time I didn't think I would ever get home." Abruptly anger welled up inside her again. "And what did I come back to? My husband's engagement party!"

"Cassa, I—"

"Get out of here. Don't ever walk in on me again." She turned off the water and struggled to wrap a towel around her body. "You shouldn't have invaded my privacy."

"I'm sorry." He shrugged, then looked back at her. "If you like, I can stop back later to pick you up. I have to swing by Mansard's to pick up some carpets they tried out on the floor. I could come back and take you to the store if you like."

Cassa's spirits immediately lifted at the thought of having such a prestigious fur salon as Mansard's trying out their carpets. But, still angry, she retorted, "How do you know I want to go to the store?"

"Don't you?" he shot back. "I heard you talking to yourself in the shower, just like you used to do when you were getting ready to go to work. That hasn't changed. You always sang or talked in the shower." For a moment he stared at her, his eyes turning from steel blue to navy. "I know how much you've always loved the store. I can't believe that's changed either."

A wave of powerful emotion assailed Cassa as she tried to fight the attraction she had always felt for Dan. "Go away," she whispered, turning her back on him.

He sucked in a sharp breath. Even through the towel, her lovely backside brought an ache to his loins. "You're so beautiful," he murmured half to himself as Cassa whipped around to face him again.

"What did you say?" she demanded.

"Nothing. I'll call later to see if you want me to pick you up." He left the bathroom, closing the door behind him.

Cassa stood where she was, staring at the closed door, feeling as if Dan's look had scorched her with fire and cooled her with ice. It had always been like that between them, but to experience the sensation again after so long was overwhelming.

As she applied lipstick, the only makeup she owned, she cursed herself for being moved by Dan. After all, he'd betrayed her with another woman . . .

Cassa dressed in Maddy's lavender jeans and a beige silk shirt and regarded her image in the mirror. "You look as if you've just come from a rummage sale." She shook her head at the scruffy sneakers she'd discovered in the back of the guest closet. "At least Carla didn't find these."

She descended the stairs to the foyer and entered the kitchen, where she found two slices of toast under a silver cover and freshly brewed coffee in the pot. "I'm alive and I'm home," she sang aloud, relishing the still-hot toast and coffee.

Cassa left a note for Mrs. Bills to prepare dinner as usual. She assumed that Dan was still employing the housekeeper, who came every morning at nine and left after preparing the evening meal. Cassa didn't try to explain her reappearance in the note, but she told the woman she would speak with her as soon as possible.

She signed her name with a flourish, trying not to think what she would do if Dan already had a dinner engagement—with Carla—and placed the note on the countertop under the antique trivet she and Dan had found in an old barn in Seneca County. She paused briefly, remembering their trip together, then rinsed her cup and ran upstairs to brush her teeth, slowing down as a slight vertigo briefly assailed her.

She was in good shape; she had exercised all the time she'd been in Suwanon, and although the food had not been plentiful, an abundance of nutritious figs, dates, and oranges had kept her fairly healthy.

She stepped out the front door into a sunny late May morning, inhaling the perfume of the fresh breeze and admiring the fluffy clouds in the blue sky and the new green leaves on the trees that lined the narrow street. Lilacs, the city flower, bloomed in every yard.

Cassa slowly began to jog toward the center of town, feeling a bit uneasy as soon as she left the historical district and crossed the bridge over the expressway leading to the business section. At first, she didn't look at other joggers or smile at anyone as she always had in the past on her way to work. She'd developed the habit of avoiding any kind of direct confrontation in prison—especially with the guards—and it stayed with her now.

When she reached the bridge over the Genesee River she began to feel somewhat more relaxed, and she paused to stare into the turbulent water, which was dotted here and there with logs and tree stumps. Through the noise of traffic she thought she heard the rush of the Upper Falls a quarter of a mile away. Could it be? Maybe, maybe not. With a smile she resumed her walk.

A few moments later Cassa realized she was being followed. Fearfully she glanced over her shoulder but didn't recognize the Mercedes Sports Coup cruising close to the curb. She looked again. Was that Dan's face behind those sunglasses?

The car pulled to a stop, blocking traffic, and Dan jumped out to the accompaniment of horns blasting and irate drivers shouting. He stepped up on the curb next to her. "Get in the car, Cassa. You're tired."

"I'm just fine," she disagreed. Then, looking over his shoulder, she added, "But if I'm not mistaken, you aren't. There seems to be a mounted patrolman coming to arrest you for obstructing traffic."

Dan followed her gaze. "So there does." He looked back

at her. "Please get in the car," he said softly, but with a hint of steel, "or I'll throw you over my shoulder and let him arrest me for kidnapping."

"You can't threaten me," Cassa retorted, watching the grim-faced police officer weaving past the backed-up cars toward them. "All right, all right, let's go. But don't think you can intimidate me."

"The shoe is on the other foot, I think." Dan helped her into the car, nonchalantly waved to the policeman, and slid behind the wheel, ignoring the blare of horns behind them.

"You never used to be so inconsiderate of other people," Cassa stated flatly, staring out the passenger window. "And when did you decide to get a sports car? Was Carla impressed?" She raised her chin proudly. Damn him.

"I'm not inconsiderate of people. I didn't want you to tire yourself. That's important to me." Dan threw a quick glance at her. "And I bought the car for many reasons, none of them involving Carla."

"Bull," Cassa replied, and fell silent as his hands tightened on the wheel.

Inside, Dan was seething. Damn you, my darling, he raged to himself; don't you know I used a million diversionary tactics to stay alive, once I found you were gone from me? One of these days, when he had Cassa's trust again, he'd explain about all the futile things he'd done to keep from going mad without her.

The silence between them grew tense and heavy. Each time Cassa swallowed, the sound echoed in the small enclosure.

It required several horn-blowing, brake squealing minutes for them to get to East Avenue, where they turned down the alley that led to the parking area behind Tijanian's. Cassa opened the door and stepped onto the pavement, pausing a moment to take in the medley of sounds around her. The Christ Church carillon struck the hour. Students at the Eastman School were tuning up their instruments. It was just as she'd remembered. Cassa couldn't suppress a grin of pleasure. She glanced over the top of the car at Dan. "The same sounds."

Much is the same, my lamb, he thought. I love you more than life . . . as I always have.

Not moving, Cassa watched him. "What you said before about the shoe being on the other foot . . ." She cleared her throat. "I suppose you meant that I intimidate you."

Dan stared back, his face expressionless. He wanted to sweep her into his arms and never let her go, but he knew he would have to proceed slowly. "We have a great deal to discuss, Cassa, but here, in Parson's Alley, is not the place." He slowly started across the narrow street to the back door of Tijanian's. In large letters a sign on the door warned that the building was protected by guard dogs.

Cassa remained where she was, enjoying the crisp spring day, the bustle of traffic on East Avenue, the cacaphony from the music school. "They're resurfacing the brick in the old Rochester Club," she announced to no one in particular.

Realizing that Dan was holding the door open for her, she crossed to him. "I see we still use the guard dogs," she said, automatically visualizing the many one-of-a-kind carpets in the shop, the invaluable rugs that made up their inventory.

"Yes." Dan took a deep breath as she accompanied him inside, the smell of her shampoo making him dizzy with desire. "I'm sure the dogs were picked up earlier, as usual. We're still the only ones with keys to the store. I kept your set in the safety deposit box."

"You didn't give those to the Salvation Army? How sentimental of you," she said sarcastically.

"Dammit, Cassa!" He cursed louder as the phone rang, and glaring at her, he strode to the desk, lifted the receiver, and barked "Yes?"

Cassa wandered past the twin rolltop desks that she and Dan had purchased at an auction, over the Heriz rug that covered most of the oak floor, and paused on the threshold of the showroom. Dry sobs wracked her throat as she stared around her. If only Uncle Aram were here now.

She stared up at the antique Kerman rug hanging on the wall, its soft blues, pinks, and creams giving life to the stark wooden walls and floors. Her eyes turned to the ruby Sarouk with its jewel center and floral motif. She drew strength from the richness and serenity of her surroundings. This was home. This had always been the one place where she could completely lose herself—hide, escape, heal, and then return to everyday life. Even as a child she'd often come to lie upon the vibrant carpets and imagine herself in the time of Aladdin and the Arabian Nights.

She stroked the rolled-up carpets, her fingers searching and finding the knots, automatically registering the fact that the Isfahan at her feet was a very fine rug indeed.

"Feel good?" Dan asked behind her.

She nodded without turning.

"Won't you be too tired to work today?" he asked softly.

She shrugged. "Do I still have a place here?"

"Damn you, Cassa, of course you have a place here. This is our business. We've built it up together. It belongs to both of us."

She nodded. "I'd like to put in a few hours today, but I think, for now, I'll walk over to the Y. Maddy called early this morning to tell me she's arranged for me to use the facility, and my muscles feel a little stiff today. After that, I think I'll walk over to her shop."

"I have a meeting this morning, otherwise I'd walk you to the Y. I have a membership."

"You do?" Cassa was surprised. Dan was a golfer, an occasional jogger, and now and then a tennis player, but he had always disliked swimming and any kind of regimented exercise.

He felt his face flush as he nodded. What the hell did she think he'd done, with her gone? If he hadn't worked out at the gym to the point of exhaustion, he would have gone mad.

"When do you have time to golf at the club if—?"

"I haven't been to Birch Hill in months," Dan interrupted, thinking: I saw you behind every tree on that course, Cassa mine. I heard your laugh whenever the birds sang. I would have put a bullet through my head if I'd hung around there without you.

Cassa stared open-mouthed as he whirled away from her and stormed through the office and out the back door. She blinked as the door banged shut, rattling a row of oriental spice jars on a shelf. She and Dan had bought them on their honeymoon trip, in Kyoto, the ancient capital of Japan.

Now she stared at the slammed door. Why was Dan so angry? It was she who'd been betrayed. As she straightened the spice jars, she muttered, "If he had broken these, I would have sued him."

The door to the back room opened and footsteps came toward her from the office. "Cassa, my dear, is it really you?" a familiar voice cried. "I saw Maddy this morning, and she told me, but I didn't believe it."

A slight, dark man held out his arms, and Cassa walked straight into them. It was Dendor Parnisian, an old friend of her Uncle Aram, who had retired from his law practice years ago. Every day since then he'd worked in the shop as a salesman, accepting only minimum wages for his efforts because it made him happy just to be among such beautiful reminders of his native Turkey.

"Darling Dendor, were you terribly shocked?" Cassa patted the swarthy man's thin back. Dendor had always been like a member of her family. She leaned away from him, knowing her eyes were as moist as his. "It's good to be home. Shall we have some coffee?"

"Of course. It will be ready in a few minutes."

Cassa sat in her office chair and watched the old Armenian prepare the thick Turkish coffee. He poured the brew into delicate thimble-sized china cups with an oriental design and set out matching plates piled high with tiny honey cakes.

Cassa took delight in the ritual. She remembered the stories Dendor had told her about his family, many of whom had died in the massacres of 1915, when the Turks killed thousands of Armenians. Dendor had escaped, thanks to an aunt who had taken him to France. He spoke seven languages, cherished the traditions of his own culture, and revered the customs of other people.

He and Cassa spoke quietly, touching only briefly on her painful experience. Mostly she asked him how he'd been getting on. Finally and reluctantly she got up to leave, mentioning her plan to swim at the Y.

Dendor took the cup from her hand and pulled her to her feet. "Of course you must go." He patted her hand. "Life seems strange to you now, even alien, but you will find your place, child, given time. You must wrestle with demons as we all do. It is the wise man who trains for combat. Work out your problems while you work out your body, child." His rich velvet-brown eyes seemed to be looking deep into her very soul. "You will win, my friend of many years." He nodded and left her, a faraway look in his wise eyes.

Cassa stared after him, considering his words. Then she hefted her oversized purse, which contained a swimsuit and towel, and set off the for Y, thinking: I'm home again, and free to make my own choices.

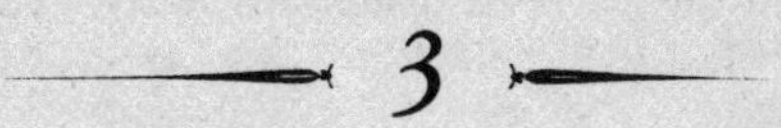

ONCE OUTSIDE IN Parson's Alley, Cassa paused to take a deep breath and look behind her. There were no guards!

She strode down the narrow passageway to Gibb's Street, increasing her pace as she walked past Kilbourn Hall and the Eastman Theater to Main Street, where she waited at the corner for the light to change, then crossed to the new Metro Center.

Inside, she inquired about a membership and showed her guest pass. She casually toured the facility, from the first floor to the third, watching the handball and racquetball players, the weight-watchers, and the runners. When she felt a bit stronger, she'd work out with the weights.

She was heading for the locker room to change into her swimsuit when one of the women at the front desk approached her.

"Mrs. Welles, your husband just called and asked us to remind you to use the hot tub and steam room."

"Thank you, I will if I have time," she said, wondering why he had bothered to call about that.

She chose a locker, changed her clothes, and secured her

belongings inside. Now, how did she get to the pool? "Just follow the arrows," she muttered to herself.

"Did you ask where the pool is?" an elderly woman said, staring at Cassa like a bright bird. "I'm Florence Carnock, and I'm in the exercise class."

"How nice."

"Follow the signs. You'll find the pool."

"Thank you."

"Young people these days have no common sense," Florence grumbled under her breath, stuffing her round body into tights and a leotard. "Must be all that pot-smoking." Her gluteus maximus quivering, she sailed past an outraged Cassa. "Every home is an opium den today," the senior citizen opined, a little louder this time, as she exited the locker room.

"Bull," Cassa mumbled, grimacing at herself in the mirror. She'd lost weight in every part of her body—everywhere but the one place she wanted to lose it. Cassa had always wished she were flat-chested and athletic-looking, rather than full-breasted. But that no longer seemed very important. She was alive, and that was all that mattered. She smiled into the mirror before leaving the room.

Cassa had no trouble finding the pool, which was almost empty. One swimmer was thrashing up and down his lane like a finalist in the Olympics.

Cassa fitted her goggles and cap to her head, lowered herself into the cool water, and began her slow but steady crawl. After ten lengths of the pool, she was winded and had to stop. But after resting for a few moments she began again and managed to swim another five lengths before exhaustion overcame her. She'd had enough. She leaned her head and arms on the pool's concrete rim, then climbed out, feeling pleasantly tired. The fearful anxiety that had accompanied her for the last nine months was beginning to melt away.

She asked a guard where the hot tub was and followed his directions to an area just off the pool. She was sitting alone in the large pool of swirling water, her eyes closed, her body swaying freely, when a rush of cold air told her that someone else had entered the room.

Suddenly she felt a hand on her back lifting her away from the tile-lined bath. Her eyes flew open and her body stiffened. "You!" she gasped, water splashing into her mouth. "I thought you were at a meeting."

"It didn't last long," Dan answered, his body sliding under hers, making the hot tub seem several degrees warmer.

"Stop that. People will see." Cassa glanced anxiously at the huge expanse of windows that opened onto the sauna on one side and the pool on the other, allowing the lifeguard who patrolled the pool an unobstructed view of the whole area.

Then, as Dan slipped his hand down the back of her bathing suit, she stopped worrying about who might be watching. His fingers gently kneaded her buttocks as she floated lazily in the bubbling water.

"When I thought you were dead, it was as though someone had turned a light out inside of me." Dan said quietly, his voice echoing slightly in the concrete room.

"How long did that feeling last—a day?" Cassa asked, but she was too relaxed to generate the sarcasm and anger she was feeling and she cursed herself for not socking Dan in the jaw right then.

"I needed you, Cassa. I always have . . . from the first moment I realized that the sweet little girl I knew had grown into a very lovely young lady, and that I had to marry her. I couldn't wait more than a few months, love."

"Bull," Cassa squawked as she tried to ignore the hand caressing her body. "If you needed me so much—"

"I needed you then. I need you now," Dan interrupted roughly. "Even when you were a baby—"

"I was fifteen when you met me, remember? That's not exactly a baby."

"You were a baby, but I thought you were cute, and I liked having you around—even when we played football." Dan's chuckle quavered, and his hand tightened on her bottom, bringing her closer to him. His mouth parted as it approached hers.

Just then a potbellied man pushed open the pool door and headed straight for the hot tub. They pushed apart abruptly as he ambled down the three steps into the water, setting himself just inches away from Dan and Cassa.

Dan muttered an imprecation and surged to his feet. "I'll see you at Maddy's later," he told Cassa.

"Did you call this woman a bastard?" the potbellied man called after the departing Dan. "Cause if you did..." He turned to Cassa. "I was going to tell him where to go."

Cassa smiled innocently at the man. "You must have a death wish," she said pleasantly, rising. Then she, too, got out of the tub.

"You come here every day?" the man inquired.

"No." She rinsed herself off under the wall shower and left, ignoring the fat man's suggestion that they get together some evening.

Cassa returned to the locker room, where another woman directed her to the steambath. But sitting in the clouds of moist heat made her feel claustrophobic, and she quickly returned to the regular shower room to wash her hair.

A tentative sense of well-being pulsed through her as she set out for Maddy's salon in the Midtown Mall several blocks away. Cassa strolled down Main Street, passing familiar landmarks and observing the traffic with renewed interest. She wondered if these people knew how lucky they were to be free to drive their cars where they pleased, to walk anywhere, to say whatever was on their mind.

She passed the Liberty Pole, a downtown monument, crossed the wide street to the mall, and paused in front of a shop with the name MADDY'S emblazoned on the sparkling windows. Everyone except Len and Dan had told Maddy it was foolish to open a small dress shop so close to several department stores, but Maddy's business had thrived from the day she'd first opened it—thanks in part to the talented Girardot LeBlanc, who had been a classmate of Cassa's at the Rochester Institute of Technology. He was fast becoming a well-respected designer of women's clothes. His artistic abilities and Maddy's business know-how made them ideal partners.

Cassa used her key to open the front door and entered the shop, which was decorated with understated elegance in champagne and beige silks. "Maddy?" Cassa called, then grinned when a short, dapper man exploded from the back room. "Gerry!" she squealed as he gave her a big hug and a kiss.

"Will you stop calling me Gerry! You're ruining my image as a French couturier," he scolded, wiping his eyes.

"Quebecois couturier," Cassa shot back, kissing him.

"Would you mind not making love to my partner?" Maddy teased from the doorway. "Gir has been getting out all his original samples for you to try on. Wasn't I right, Gir? Isn't she beautifully thin?"

He nodded enthusiastically. "Yes. The samples will fit perfectly. Lord, you're a rail, child. What did they do to you?"

"I'm hardly your child," Cassa pointed out. "I'm just six months younger than you."

"But much like a child, nonetheless," Gir claimed loftily.

Cassa pretended to glare at him, then answered his question. "Nothing was done to me, really. We were kept in a guarded house with a small walled-in yard where I walked and jogged in place." She swallowed dryly as the painful memories returned.

Before Gir or Maddy could respond, someone knocked on the door. Gir opened it wide, and Len entered. Cassa smiled and Maddy blushed.

"Hello." He kissed his sister and turned almost at once to Maddy. "I wanted to see if I could buy you anything . . . Cassa, I mean."

"Of course," Maddy answered in a colorless voice.

"Come, child, it's time to get you out of those hand-me-downs," Gir urged.

"Those happen to be *my* clothes," Maddy protested.

"Well, they don't suit Cassa at all. You stay here and talk to your husband." Gir flapped his hands and then pulled Cassa through the curtains, leaving Maddy and Len open-mouthed behind him. "It's about time those two talked. I'd like to know why the hell it's taken him so long to come to see her."

"Both Maddy and Len are very proud," Cassa whispered, wishing Gir would lower his voice.

"Stubborn, you mean," he replied testily. "I can't stand the way she mopes around all the time, pretending to enjoy that dentist's company. And when I see Len, he always has a double martini in his hand." Gir glowered at Cassa. "Still, I suppose we ought to mind our own business."

"Since when have you ever done that?" Cassa teased, earning another dark look from her dear friend. "Now, Ger—I mean Gir—about the clothes. I don't want—"

"Cassa, my love, I do not attempt to instruct you on your oriental rugs." He sniffed haughtily. "So please don't try to tell me about clothes." With that he strode ahead of her to his workroom. Cassa was about to follow when a white-faced Maddy stepped past the curtains.

"Maddy, I know the discreet thing would be to say nothing, but you're more a sister than a sister-in-law to me, and Len says there's trouble between you. How can you two let all you had together just slip away?"

"Erode away would be a better word for it, I think," Maddy said grimly, her face pale and drawn. "There's too much pain between us, Cass."

"Is he gone?"

"No." Maddy's smile was fleeting. "He's picking out lingerie for his baby sister."

"Good grief. Please go and help him, Mad. You know what a terrible sense of color he has."

"You mean because he's wearing dark blue socks with that green suit?"

"Is he? I didn't notice." Cassa put a hand to her mouth in mock shock.

"Yes. I used to mark all his clothes with numbers so he—" Maddy stopped abruptly and pressed her lips together in a hard line. Then, shaking her head at Cassa, she went back through the curtains and into the store.

Cassa turned to see Girardot gesticulating from his workroom. "For God's sake, will you get moving, Cass! Madeleine will get the coffee," he instructed, apparently unaware that Maddy was no longer there to hear him.

"Mais oui, mon empereur," Cassa replied with a smile before relaying the order to Maddy, who was standing next to Len as he studied a rainbow of lingerie.

Both Len and Maddy laughed, used to Gir's ways, then returned to an intense consideration of the proper underwear for Cassa.

She watched them for a while before quietly retracing her steps. From Gir's workshop she heard an impatient cough. "Over here, Cass," he hissed, "and stop ogling my clothes like a designer pirate."

Gir pulled her onto a circular section of brown parquet tile, and for the next hour Cassa was turned, twisted, pinned, pushed, groaned and exclaimed over, and generally manhandled until she wanted to tell Girardot to shove his creations up a chimney.

"Almost done," he grumbled. "Really, Cass, you can be very trying." He dragged a length of soft cotton from around her body, spinning her like a top.

"Me? Trying?" Cassa glared at him, standing in her briefs and bra, arms akimbo, furious with his overbearing ways but happy, too, because she was back home, arguing with him again.

Girardot had drawn himself up to his full five feet five and was just opening his mouth to make a retort, when suddenly Dan stuck his head into the room and barked, "Get dressed, Cassa. Now!"

Dan's angry words ricocheted off the walls like bullets. His expression was as dark and hard as a bronze sculpture of Lucifer. It tore him apart to see his wife half-dressed in front of Girardot, though reason told him Gir had seen her that way many times before while fitting her for clothes. All Dan knew was that he could have killed the man for looking at her.

Cassa opened her mouth to tell Dan she had been strip-searched more than once in Suwanon, that she had modeled for Gir and other art students at school with even less on, but one look at his furious face changed her mind. She accepted the dressing gown Girardot handed her and said, "Listen, Dan—"

"LeBlanc, if I ever find you and my wife . . ." Dan moved forward as he enunciated each syllable. Even as he spoke, he knew he was acting like a fool; but since Cassa's return he'd been overreacting to everything. Fierce possessiveness, and an even more powerful protectiveness, dictated his actions.

"Watch it, Welles," the spunky Gir warned, then flushed, irritation flashing across his face. Cassa knew it was Dan's calling him by his last name, which he never used anymore, rather than the insinuation that was really upsetting the temperamental artist.

"Wait a minute," Cassa interjected, feeling her own anger take hold. "What right do you have to come roaring in here like some wronged—"

"What right?" Dan bellowed, stunning Cassa with his wrath. Her husband rarely lost control like this.

Inside, Dan was thinking: You're mine, Cassa, mine. And you and everyone else had better not forget it!

"Shhh!" Maddy came running toward them from the main store. "I have two customers out there who think we've been invaded by Martians." Panting, she glowered at all three of them. "Gir, come out front with me. One of the women is asking for you."

"Very well, but"—he pointed a finger at Dan—"don't think I'm afraid of you, you rug-selling behemoth, because I'm not." He turned to Cassa, taking deep breaths to calm himself. "Darling, all the things I fitted to you are perfect, of course. I think you should take them all. Shall I choose the accessories?"

"No," Cassa said firmly. "And I don't need all those clothes."

"Yes, you do," Dan snapped, scowling at Gir. "Whatever fits her, we're taking. We'll buy the accessories ourselves." His eyes flashed as he warned Cassa, "And I don't want any arguments from you."

"Suit yourselves, then." Gir shrugged and followed Maddy, mumbling something about crazy husbands in fitting rooms.

Cassa was stunned by Dan's display. She'd never seen him that way before. In happier times he'd just smiled proudly when other men flirted with her. He hadn't minded a bit, because he'd always known how much she loved him. How they had chuckled together after returning home from a club get-together, each of them describing in detail the toe-tromping they'd received from inept dancers. Neither she nor Dan had ever been jealous. Their trust in each other had been unshakable. But now everything seemed to have changed.

Cassa shook her head to clear it of disturbing thoughts

and tightened the tie of the dressing gown around her waist. She fixed her eyes on a point just past Dan's shoulder. "He's right. You shouldn't be here."

"And you shouldn't be almost nude," Dan snarled, his body tensed for action. He wanted to take apart the building, brick by brick.

"My underwear covers me more than the bikini you always told me was so sexy." Cassa lowered her voice when she remembered the customers in the front room.

"I'm your husband," Dan fired back. "It's all right for me to see you like that."

Cassa was seething. How dare he dictate to her. She was free now, and not about to exchange one prison for another. Anger made her speak without thinking. "Hah!" she cried. "You would have loved the way the Suwanese soldiers elbowed each other aside to watch one of their women strip-search us. Sometimes the women thought it was funny, and didn't close the door." Cassa gulped, raising her clenched fists to cover her mouth. Why had she resurrected those memories when all she wanted to do was bury them? She was in agony, but she couldn't stop. "And the men would stand there laughing."

Dan's face went suddenly pale. "Oh my God, darling." In an instant he was at her side, folding her gently in his arms, his body curving protectively around hers. "I can't bear to think of you going through such a thing. I could kill them all for what they did to you."

Deep inside he was wracked with painful images of terror and violation. They'd assaulted her! The fearful possibility that had lay waiting since she'd first returned to him exploded into a horrible reality. She was still hiding it from him, but he knew she'd been raped. At the mere thought, Dan died a little. The pain! The horror! But no one would ever hurt her again. He wouldn't let her dwell on what had happened. He'd fill her life with peace and beauty.

Cassa fought the warm, languid feelings stealing over her as Dan sheltered her in his embrace. Her brain ordered her arms to push him away, but instead they stole around his waist and clasped him tightly to her. Delight coursed through her veins as she felt his lips leave her hair and travel down the side of her face to nibble at the corner of her mouth. A sensation of homecoming bloomed like May lilacs inside her. He was her security, her comfort, her tall, muscular husband, who looked more like a triathlon contender than a rug merchant. Her heart rolled over and her soul melted with yearning as she looked into his beautiful blue eyes. She wanted to make love with him right then and there.

"I'll never let you take another trip away from me. I won't let you leave town, let alone leave the country, unless I'm beside you every step of the way." Dan's heart turned to ice as he once more imagined all she'd suffered. His mouth closed over hers, taking, claiming, entering, belonging. "No one will ever hurt you again," he growled, drawing away for a moment before kissing her again.

The touch of their tongues heated their bodies to fever pitch. Without thinking, she moved against him in the sweet, remembered way. When she heard him groan her name, life seemed to flow into her again. The last vestiges of fear melted away. Her mind and spirit opened like a rose bud petal to the sun.

"I'll never let you out of my sight," Dan mumbled, his mouth still holding hers, the movement of his lips stirring a wild, sensual need that roared deep within her very being.

But even in her joyful haze, the vivid memory of Carla smiling up at Dan returned to Cassa with breathtaking force. Her hands clenched at Dan's waist, then lifted and pushed hard against his chest. "Don't you think Carla might object?" she said scathingly.

"What?" Dan looked down at her, his eyes glazed.

Just then Maddy swept into the room. "So what have you decided? Ooops! Sorry." And she began backing away.

"No. Wait, Maddy." Cassa's voice sounded shrill in the sudden silence. "I'm not going to take all the clothes Gir laid out for me." Pushing herself out of Dan's arms, she gestured toward the articles filling the clothes rack and scattered over the table, at the work area overflowing with drawing and swatches of materials.

Dan stared at her intently for a moment, then walked over to the worktable. "These are good, Maddy, and they will suit Cassa perfectly," he said. "Tell Girardot I've bought them all." He turned swiftly, catching Cassa staring at him, and pointed to a peach linen suit. "She might want to wear that now."

"No—" Cassa stopped as his face twisted with fury. "I . . . I mean I can't wear the suit without shoes and a slip." She raised her chin, summoning up the courage to meet Dan's fiery blue eyes.

He nodded once, and grasped her wrist with steely fingers. "Tell Girardot we'll take the suit with us and that we'll want the first outfit he's sewing by the third Saturday of June, when we go to the Birch Hill dance."

Cassa opened her mouth to tell him she didn't want anything to do with the club. Suddenly the place that had been the center of their social activities had ceased to appeal to her. A fireplace with just the two of them before it was all she wanted now.

"Good Lord," Maddy said, slapping her forehead, "I completely forgot about the dance, and Jack will be out of town that weekend."

"Come with us," Dan offered casually, glancing at Cassa and noting the rebellious tilt of her jaw. "You won't mind if Maddy rides with us, will you, love?"

Seeing the amused luster in his eyes, Cassa glared at him. He had backed her into a corner. "No, of course I don't mind, if—"

"Good. I knew you'd feel that way. Now let's get out of here." He pulled her gently, but she was caught off-balance and almost fell into his arms. Hardly waiting for her to regain her footing, he urged her down the corridor.

"Wait!" Maddy called after them. "Girardot is going to the dance, and I know he doesn't have a date."

Dan shot her an irritated look. "All right. Bring him along." He pulled Cassa after him down the hall.

"Damn you, Dan," Cassa muttered. "What do you think I am—a trailer?"

As they burst into the main area of the store, Cassa still trying to free herself, five women shoppers turned to stare at them. Dan's teeth flashed in a smile. "My wife is pregnant," he explained. At Cassa's gasp his grin widened. "She's acting testy because she doesn't feel well."

"I know how it is," said one of the women, holding a

dress up in front of her. "I was an absolute bear for nine months."

"Great!" Cassa muttered as Gir, who had been talking to another woman, came hurrying toward them, his mouth open. "Now look what you've done," Cassa squeaked to Dan. "He'll ask me a million questions."

Ignoring Gir's approach, Dan pulled Cassa through the door to the mall, and past store after store. She puffed along beside him, trying to pry her arm free while protesting against his manhandling. She took a deep breath and indignantly announced, "I have never been testy in my life, and I certainly am not pregnant."

"But do you agree that you could become testy if you did get pregnant?"

"It could happen, yes, but that's not the issue." Cassa almost plowed into an elderly woman in a flowered hat with a bulging shopping bag as Dan made a sharp right turn into a department store. "Pardon me," Cassa shouted over her shoulder.

The old woman glared at them. "You wanna fool around, get a room. I'm sick of you youngsters making love in the mall." She ran after them and jabbed her umbrella into Dan's leg. "In my day we did that stuff in beds, not on benches."

"Right you are, ma'am," Dan said, reaching down to rub his thigh. "And as soon as I buy this woman some presents, I'll take her home and make love to her."

"Oh?" The old lady's eyebrows shot up. "She one of those you gotta pay? Why, young fella, you look good enough to get it for nuthin'." The harridan cackled merrily as she went on her way.

"Now, see here—" Cassa sputtered.

"Come along, darling." Dan led her down several steps into the store and along an aisle to the shoe department.

For the next forty minutes Cassa was fitted with an assortment of low-heeled, high-heeled, dressy, and sport footwear. Not all of her muttered protests halted the flow of shoes from the back room.

"We can't afford this," Cassa whispered to Dan as she watched the pile of boxes grow.

"We can afford it," he replied with a shrug. "You once told me the brand of shoes they sell here is the most comfortable for you," he added, signaling the salesman to add yet another box to the assortment.

"True, but I don't buy all my shoes here. Think of the expense."

"Dammit, Cassa, hang the expense," Dan retorted, bringing the salesman's head up. Silently he added: All those months you were gone, I remembered how I'd shopped for presents for you. I felt a knife twisting in my heart every time I walked past a woman's store. It cut me up to see a jeweler's display and think that I would never again pick out something for you. He smiled as she stared at him, open-mouthed. She was just beginning to realize what he'd gone through when he thought he'd lost her.

When they finally left the shoe department they were carrying not only the peach linen suit, but also low-heeled bone slings and a matching leather purse to wear with it. The rest of their purchases would be picked up later by Freddy, who had driven the Tijanian delivery truck for years.

Next Dan escorted Cassa up an escalator to the lingerie department.

Cassa was stunned. "I don't believe this! You always made me buy my own nighties because you said it made you uncomfortable to visit the lingerie section."

A dark blush crept up his face. "I've changed."

"Changed isn't the word," Cassa mumbled as she inspected a sheer wisp of apricot silk.

Dan took it from her, his blue eyes warming as he glanced from the camisole to Cassa and back again. "We'll take it," he told the plump woman behind the counter.

Dan's enthusiasm seemed boundless. He approved of innumerable articles of sleepwear and undies, all in the softest pastels.

"You're not outfitting a seraglio," Cassa reminded him, tugging at his suit sleeve while the gleeful saleslady beamed at them both.

"Huh?" Dan asked absentmindedly, running his fingers over a black silk slip. "Don't be a spoilsport, darling. I'm finding this very enjoyable."

"Let's go. That's enough."

"In a minute. Let me see that lavender teddy."

"You seem awfully well versed in the terminology,"

Cassa commented dryly. "You used to think a teddy was something a child took to bed."

Dan looked down at her, his eyes warming her, riveting her, loving her.

"You could be arrested for . . . for looking at people like that." Cassa gasped, and turned away to gaze blindly at the shoppers passing by.

"People? I wasn't looking at people; I was looking at my wife," Dan whispered in her ear, his breath lifting the fine hair at the nape of her neck and making her shiver. "Cold, darling?" He pulled her close to his side and told the saleswoman to ring up their selections.

Dan took Cassa's arm again as they left the store, both of them laden with boxes and bags. Again, most of their purchases would be picked up by Freddy.

Dan strode rapidly through the mall, heading toward the underground garage.

"When did you park your car here?" Cassa asked, puffing at his side.

"After my appointment this morning I decided that this would be the easiest place to get to when you finished shopping at Maddy's." Dan shrugged, moving effortlessly through the surging throng.

Cassa bumped into a few people, the bulky parcels impeding her progress. When another irate shopper glared at her, Dan turned to Cassa, amusement curving his strong mouth, and said, "Cassa, my love, you're bouncing off everyone."

"Am not," Cassa retorted, just missing a delivery boy chewing a huge wad of gum.

Dan didn't release her arm again until he had paid the parking attendent and led her to his Mercedes.

"Do you always park miles away from anyone else, in the farthest corner of the garage?" Cassa demanded, winded.

"I haven't had this car long enough to be willing to cope with the scratches or dents I could pick up over there." Dan jerked his head toward the other cars. After stowing the boxes and bags in the trunk, he helped her into the passenger seat.

The engine sounded louder than normal in the confined area. Cassa closed her eyes as Dan peeled out of his parking place and sped down tunnels and up ramps. "For someone so worried about scratches and dents, you don't seem to mind courting collisions," she observed dryly.

"I'm careful, but I'm not a turtle." Dan scowled at her, reminding Cassa that he had never appreciated anyone questioning his driving.

"Certainly not a turtle. More like a March hare," she muttered.

"Watch it, Mrs. Welles. If I'm as crazy as you think"—he regarded her lazily—"I might bite."

Cassa cast around for a quelling retort, but nothing came to mind. She stared out the window, not speaking as they drove the short distance across the river and home to Cornhill.

While Dan got their packages out of the car, Cassa ran up the steps, using the key he'd reclaimed from the safety deposit box to open the door. She turned toward him just as the delivery truck from their store pulled up in front of the house. "It's Freddy, so soon," Cassa said, holding open the door as Dan struggled through with their boxes and bags.

He grinned at her. "I told him to give your things top priority unless he wanted you to become the Naughty Nudie of Cornhill."

"You didn't say that." Cassa laughed, aghast to think that the loyal employee she had known since childhood might have heard such a remark from her husband.

Dan's grin widened as he watched expressions of skepticism, amusement, and shock flit across her face. His dimples deepened on either side of his mouth.

"You still have them," Cassa whispered.

"Have what, darling?" Dan moved closer to her in the foyer, the door open behind them. "I still have what?" His mouth fastened to the corner of hers, his teeth nipping at her lower lip.

"Dimples," Cassa squeaked, her limbs turning numb, her eyes watering, unable to control the familiar debilitating effect Dan was having on her.

A cough coming from the open door made Cassa jump and try to push away from Dan, but he refused to release her.

Nonchalantly Dan looked over his shoulder and said,

"Freddy, how are you? Just leave the parcels in the hall. Mrs. Welles and I will take them upstairs. Say hello to Mary and the grandchildren for me."

"Hello, Freddy," Cassa said from the circle of Dan's arms, feeling color flood her face when her husband continued to nuzzle her neck, his eyes half closed.

Freddy Bates beamed at her, then gave her a hug when she finally managed to free herself from Dan's hold. "The missus and me was glad to see you returned to us from them foreigners, Miss Cassa."

"Thank you, Freddy. And thank you for bringing my things. Dan!" Cassa gasped as her husband pulled her back into his arms. "And . . . and say hello to Mary for me."

"That I will." Freddy didn't seem the least embarrassed by Dan'a affectionate display. "I'll be seeing you at the store. It's a good thing you're back . . . for everybody's sake." He looked at Dan, laughed, and left.

Dan nudged the door shut with his foot, still holding Cassa tight.

"That wasn't very polite of you," she managed to say as his hand went to the buttons of her blouse.

"I'll apologize . . . later," he muttered, his fingers sliding under the silk, then up and over her breasts, kneading them gently. "It's been so long, sweetheart, so long since I've touched your beautiful breasts." His breath grew ragged, and his heart seemed about to burst from his chest.

"You're engaged to Carla." Cassa didn't want to think about the woman whose face had suddenly intruded into her mind.

"Wrong. I'm a married man . . . and you're"—Dan bent and swiftly, powerfully, scooped her up in his arms—"the woman I married." He held her motionless, mesmerizing her with the blue fire in his eyes.

He'd betrayed her, and she should tell him to go to hell. Instead she said, "Yes, I am." She should choke him to death. Instead she raised her arms and clasped him gently around the neck.

Without taking his eyes from hers, he carried her up the floating staircase. Reason told him she might hate his touch, that she had been ravaged and might be repelled by his lovemaking. Yet nothing on earth could have stopped him from wanting her, from trying to love her, from trying to free her from the bondage of memory with his loving body, heart, and soul.

"Mrs. Bills!" Cassa suddenly gasped, remembering the housekeeper.

"I told her not to come in till late this afternoon." Dan paused, trying to control his need, waiting to see if she would repulse him. He could feel a muscle jumping at the side of his mouth, his hands clenching and unclenching on her body, then tightening when she fell silent. He entered their bedroom, his heart hammering as he sat down on the bed with Cassa in his lap. "You're so light now, so slender, my darling," he murmured huskily.

"Yes." Her lips were too soft from his kisses to stretch into a smile. "My hips can get through a door now," she said, trying to lighten the mood with a joke.

He sucked on her upper lip. "Your hips were beautiful," he said, remembering the wonderfully rounded figure he had always adored. How was it he could have thought her perfect then, yet still think she was perfect now, so slender, so fragile, so very graceful. He inhaled her clean scent, the sweet essence that had always been Cassa.

Swinging her around onto the bed, he settled himself beside her. "I want to undress you slowly, darling, to savor every minute of our love," Dan mused, his hands stilling. If she wanted him to stop, he would, he promised himself, gritting his teeth in an effort to control his full, hot arousal.

Cassa felt his hesitation. Impatiently, she pulled him to her, caressing his cheek, then dropping lower to loose his tie and unfasten the buttons on his shirt. She sighed when the shirt fell open to reveal the dark arrow of hair that extended down his chest and below his belt to the lovely lower part of his body that never ceased to excite her. Even now she remembered the many times she and Dan had cavorted naked on that bed, pleasuring each other, shutting out the rest of the world with their lovemaking. Her fingers tingled as they closed around his arousal.

Dan gasped with growing urgency. Then he slipped the blouse from her shoulders, passionately kissing her burning flesh as his pulse thundered in his ears. *Cassa! Cassa!* He frowned momentarily as he lifted his head to study the livid scar that tapered to a point just above her breasts in the front and down past her shoulder blade in the back. "They hurt you." He spat the words out of his mouth like a curse before he gathered her close again, his mouth a balm on the pink wound.

Cassa felt her lavender slacks sliding free of her body and Dan's mouth following them downward. His tongue flicked over her thighs, then down her legs to her ankles, loving every inch, then ministering to her toes and the soles of her feet, which had always been devilishly ticklish. Now they arched and flexed with a sensual life of their own.

When Dan gently turned her over on her stomach and began to caress her calves, she shivered with delight. Her heart began to beat faster and faster as she rode to a wild, wonderful place where only she and Dan could go.

His teeth nipped her derriere, and she couldn't control the sobbing gasp that rose from her throat. "Dan!"

"Yes, darling." His thick voice penetrated her hazy consciousness. "Shhh, my love, I'm going to make love to you. Do you want that?"

"Yes!" Cassa's body writhed in response to a passion she'd thought long buried.

She had always loved Dan with an unswerving devotion. Their lovemaking had been satisfying for both of them, but the fire had cooled a bit over the years as they'd turned their energies to building up the business and socializing at the club. Bit by bit the demands of the world had stolen away their precious time together. Though their love itself had never lessened, lovemaking had sometimes been set aside while they fulfilled their responsibilities. The private world they'd created on their honeymoon and during the first years of their marriage had been invaded by other people.

Were we too secure in our love for each other, Dan? Cassa wondered. Did we see the world intruding, but ignore it, considering ourselves invulnerable? The disturbing questions came unbidden to her brain.

Then all coherent thought was replaced by unbridled feeling as Dan continued to caress her, his restless urgency fueling her fire. The emotional wall that had protected her during her imprisonment began to crumble. In the heat flaring between them, courage grew, and Cassa took the lead, became the aggressor.

She flipped over on her back, pulling Dan up her body. As he began his slow, tantalizing journey, his tongue flicked gently over and between her thighs. She pulled harder at him, her hands stroking his chest and shoulders. His groan thrilled her. Blood pounded in her head as the hard, hot length of him pressed against her.

"I'm going to kiss you here," Cassa murmured, pointing at his chest. Her lips touched him, tasted him. She looked up into his passion-clouded eyes. He was watching her every move. "Then I'm going to kiss you here." She touched the corner of his mouth.

"You're teasing me," he said with a growl, pulling her onto his chest and settling back against the pillows. "Lord, darling, I hope you aren't *just* going to tease me. I'll have to take cold showers for days."

"Yes." She giggled, surprising herself. "Where did that laugh come from?" But before he could answer she was trailing her lips down his cheek, loving the feel of the lightly bristled skin on her tongue. With a deep groan, he joined his body to hers. She moaned, her body moist and open, as his velvet hardness slid in and out of her deepest recesses.

She wanted to tell him that she had dreamed of this moment every night for nine long months, that visions of their lovemaking had comforted her throughout the long ordeal. But no words came as their passions lifted them beyond words, casting them into another world where they moved freely back and forth through time and space.

Cassa finally collapsed on Dan, his heaving chest a haven she never wanted to leave. They clung together, as if by possessing each other they could keep the world away. Long moments later, Cassa tried to stifle a yawn and failed. "We should get back to the store," she said without conviction.

"Umm," Dan murmured, settling her more firmly into the curve of his arm, and pulling the goose-down quilt over them. "Very cool for May," he observed, his smile lazy as he caught her watching him. "Let's have a short nap and talk about it later." He cuddled her close, his hands running up and down her naked body under the cozy quilt. Lord, it had been so long . . . yet it was better than ever before. He hadn't expected that. Their lovemaking had always been explosive and satisfying, but this time there'd been a new dimension, as though they had stripped away another veil of life and reached a new plane of giving and loving. Cassa, my lamb, he cried—but not to her—you are my life. I was dead without you. He still couldn't bring himself to say the words aloud, but he tried to convey the thought with his tender touch.

"We won't sleep if you keep doing that," Cassa said with a sigh.

"Don't be silly. You mean you think that just because I'm massaging your body, we won't sleep? I'll bet you ten dollars we do." Dan cupped her breast in one hand and used the other to trace soft circles down her abdomen to the sweet softness between her thighs.

"Dan!"

"Okay, I owe you ten bucks." He brought her under him and began kissing her again, his mouth open on hers, giving his all, surrendering his soul in love to her. "You can't imagine how much I love kissing you."

"Thank you," Cassa answered without thinking, her hands threading through the crisp, tousled black hair that fell forward on his brow, by their loving.

His eyes were hot and searching, as was his body. Passion grew tense and fierce between them, then spilled out and flowed over them in the long-sought delight of the ages. Moist and content, they slid their bodies together, their arms tight around each other, their eyes closing as they drifted into sleep.

The ring of the telephone was a startling intrusion, a desecration. "Damn them." Dan pushed back his hair, blinking, and reached across Cassa to lift the receiver. "Yes?" he snapped.

"Why, darling, what a tiger you are," Cassa heard Carla's teasing voice. "I just wanted to remind you that we're having dinner with the Wilsons at my apartment. We made the date a month ago. Cocktails at seven. Bye, love, kiss, kiss," she sang.

Cassa sprang out of bed.

"Cassa!" Dan called as he dropped the phone into the cradle.

But she had already stalked into the bathroom, slamming the door to shut out his voice, and turning the shower on full blast so he wouldn't hear her wracking sobs through the door.

4

DAN CALLED THE Wilsons and explained why he wouldn't be joining them at Carla's apartment that evening. He called Carla back and told her the same thing. Then he spoke to Cassa through the bathroom door for almost half an hour. Placating at first, he lost patience when his gentle words evoked no response. After a time he gave up, and the house fell silent.

Dan's words rang in Cassa's mind. But when she opened the door, he was gone . . . gone from the bedroom, gone from the house.

She found his note tacked to the refrigerator door: "Take the car. See you at dinner."

Carefully she guided the Mercedes to the store, delighting in the chance to drive again. She entered Tijanian's as if it were a haven, seeking—and finding—comfort from the beautiful rugs and the sagacious Dendor.

Late that afternoon her brother arrived with a man he introduced as Charles Evans, a client and interior designer who was adding the finishing touches to the Birch Hill Country Club refurbishment.

"It's a pleasure to meet you, Mrs. Welles. I don't think we've ever met. I've only been at Birch Hill for six months, but I've heard a great deal about you, and of course I read about you in the local papers this morning. Have you seen the *Banner* article yet?"

"No, I haven't, Mr. Evans." Not for the first time Cassa wished she could just forget about Suwanon. She was distressed to hear about the newspaper piece, and wondered how many of her neighbors had already read it. Well, she thought, if I'm lucky, they won't all feel compelled to mention it to me.

Turning her thoughts back to the business at hand, she turned to Charles Evans and asked, "How may we serve you here at Tijanians's?"

"You can show me some beautiful rugs," he said with a smile. "Even if I hadn't already made up my mind to bring my business to Tijanian's, your brother would have convinced me to do so."

Len shrugged and smiled.

"Well, you've come to the right place. I don't mean to brag, but—"

"Yes, you do mean to brag, sister mine," Len said, grinning. Turning to Evans, he explained, "Tijanian's has been my sister's true love ever since she was a little girl and used to play among the rolls of carpets. When other children were outside skipping rope, Cassa was in here, learning how to count the knots per inch and recognize the quality of the dyes."

"Len!" Cassa laughed.

"Our Uncle Aram used to tell her stories about the young children with deformed fingers who weave the rugs and of the families who have been doing the work for hundreds of years, passing knowledge of the dyes, designs, and weaving techniques from mother to daughter, down through the generations." Len paused, lowering his voice to a confidential whisper. "Oriental rug weaving isn't just an art, you know. It involves all of history. It parallels the evolution of mankind!" He pointed to a Bokjara hanging on the wall, the black and cream background a startling contrast to the mauves, greens, pinks and reds of the design. "Didn't that one belong to Uncle Aram's family in Armenia, Cassa?"

"Yes, isn't it lovely?" she said enthusiastically. She welcomed the shoptalk, anything to take her thoughts away from Dan and Carla.

Leading the way through the showroom, Cassa described the specific dyes used, each indigenous to the area where the rug was made.

Nodding to an older Armenian couple she recognized as friends of Dendor, she paused beside another beautiful carpet. "And this is a Kerman," she said. "To me, these are the kings of the orientals, not just because of their jewellike designs and pastel and cream backgrounds, but also because of their warm, homey look." Cassa lifted the corner and rubbed the thick pile. "Notice the number of knots per square inch." She bent down to flip the carpet and was surprised to feel her muscles protest at the unaccustomed weight. She'd always moved the heavy carpets with no great effort.

Just as Len leaned down to help her, Dan spoke from the doorway. "Cassa, don't do that. Have Freddy or one of the boys turn the rugs over for you." She looked up to see him frowning darkly. Still crouching over the carpet, she turned to retort, but the blue lightning of his eyes silenced her. Dan was furious!

She rose slowly to her feet, brushing carpet lint from her skirt. "Charles Evans . . . Daniel Welles," she introduced them abruptly.

"I'm Cassa's husband. I think we've met." Dan shoved out his hand, trying to fight the fury that still filled him because Charles Evans was looking at Cassa with warm admiration. Dammit to hell, he was going around the bend. Before Cassa left him, he'd always been amused to find other men admiring his wife. Now he wanted to punch them. What was wrong with him?

"Of course," Charles Evans said, snapping his fingers. "Your picture is hanging in the Winner's Hall at the club. You won the Anniversary Golf Invitational a few years ago."

"Yes," Dan replied. He turned to his brother-in-law and shook his hand. "Len."

"Dan," Len replied with a smile. "I brought Charles here to choose some rugs for the club. The renovations should be complete in time for the benefit dance."

"Good," Dan said. "We're going, and we're taking Maddy and Girardot with us. It seems Dexter will be out of town then."

"Ah, yes," Len said with feigned casualness. "I talked to Maddy yesterday after you and Cassa left. We're having dinner on Thursday." Avoiding his sister's curious gaze, he leaned down to inspect a Chinese carpet in vivid blues and soft champagne, stroking it with rapt concentration.

Once again Cassa began moving among the roll-up carpets, this time signaling for Bob Marx, who helped them out after school, to unroll yet another rug for Charles's perusal.

But instead of letting Cassa continue her discussion, Dan began to answer the decorator's questions. All at once Cassa realized he was leaving her completely out of the conversation. Dan's high-handed manner was intolerable. Her hands clenching into fists, she watched him move up and down the rows of carpeting, Charles Evans in tow.

Len chuckled and leaned down to whisper, "Is that smoke I see coming out of your nose?"

"Of all the high-handed . . ." Cassa fumed.

"He's just thumping his chest a little in front of Charles," her brother said with a smile. Draping an arm around her shoulder, he added, "Dan is trying to reinstate himself into your life."

"By getting engaged to another woman?" she demanded hotly.

"No. By warning everyone else off." Len took hold of Cassa's shoulders and turned her to face him. "Get that mulish look off your face, honey. Sometimes when a man feels threatened, he has to pick up his club and defend his cave." He shook her lightly. "Try to understand."

"I am trying," Cassa answered untruthfully. She looked up at her brother. "Have you ever thought of taking your own advice?" she asked, watching him flush under her penetrating gaze. "Maddy was on the verge of telling me something this morning. It seems to me that your feelings for each other aren't really dead. On the contrary, they're very much alive."

Len shook his head and looked uneasily around the room, his jaw clenched. "You don't understand, Cassa. Maddy thinks I was unfaithful to her."

"Were you?"

"That's none of your business!" He ran a hand through his light hair, which was streaked with gray. "All right . . . I was unfaithful to Maddy once. It was a long time ago, on a business trip to Los Angeles. I told her about it, and she forgave me—at least she said she did—but every now and then she'll accuse me of being unfaithful again. We've had the damnedest arguments about it. I refuse to live with a woman who won't trust me."

"But can't you see her side of the story?" Cassa asked softly. "How would you feel if Maddy told you that *she'd* been unfaithful? Wouldn't you doubt her at times, too?" Cassa watched a stream of conflicting emotions cross her brother's face. "I know you, Len. You'd hate it. You would watch her like a hawk."

"Yes," he admitted at last. He gave a great sigh and shook his head. "But we've already been apart for a few months, Cassa."

"You did ask her out to dinner," she reminded him.

"For all I know she may be planning to marry Jack Dexter."

"You're still her husband. You aren't divorced yet."

Len swallowed. "No. No, we aren't divorced yet." His eyes looked troubled as he turned away from her and joined Dan and Charles, who were crouched in front of a ruby Sarouk.

A short time later Charles Evans pronounced himself satisfied. He gave his order to Dan, said good-bye to Cassa, and left with Len, who had grown quiet and thoughtful.

At five, Cassa shooed Dendor out the door, though the older man insisted he could lock up. Dan had left earlier with Freddy to supervise the laying of the two Isfahan and three Sarouk carpets Charles had ordered for the club with the proviso that they be laid at once. Cassa assumed Dan would ask Freddy to drop him off at the house before going home himself.

At six-thirty Cassa closed the ledger book she was working on, leaned back in her chair, and closed her eyes. She was exhausted, not just from the unaccustomed physical strain of working a full day but from the emotional strain of dealing with the tension that vibrated like an exposed live wire between her and Dan.

Suddenly she was being lifted from the chair. She stiffened instinctively, then relaxed. Again the sensation of homecoming flooded over her as Dan's arms circled her waist.

"You're tired," he crooned in her ear. "You should have gone home long ago. I left the car for you."

"How . . . how did you get back here?" Cassa pulled ineffectually at the fingers caressing her waist.

"I asked Freddy to swing by the store before going home. I wasn't sure you'd still be here. If you'd already left, I would have done some more work, then walked." He reached around her and poked at the ledger. "I see you've been logging for the day."

"Yes. I know the ledger is your department, but—"

"But nothing, my love. All of this"—his hand swept around the room—"belongs to both of us. Do whatever makes you happy." He turned her in his arms, tilting her chin up with one hand. "But I thought you hated posting the day's receipts." The flash of his smile was like summer lightning.

"I did. I do. You see . . ." Cassa paused, taking a deep breath. "When I was in Suwanon I used to pretend I was doing the books or sweeping the floor or unrolling the carpeting." She shrugged. "Anything that reminded me of home seemed to keep me sane." She felt her smile slipping off her face.

Dan's arms tightened around her body, pulling her to him, and he pressed her head into his shoulder. "Guess what we're going to do tonight." His voice was hoarse, and his breath ruffled the hair above her ear. His hands trembled as he held her close to him.

"What?" Cassa struggled to stifle a yawn as weariness engulfed her. She never used to get so tired . . .

"We're going to have cold beer and white hots and marinated cucumber-and-tomato salad. And"—he grinned down at her, his heart racing at the dreamy look on her face—"Mrs. Bills came in this afternoon and made a Black Forest cake just for you."

"Ummm, I really *am* home. Rochester picnic, here I come." Cassa couldn't control a second jaw-splitting yawn. "Can I take a nap first?"

"We'll nap together," Dan crooned.

Cassa's eyes snapped open as an unpleasant thought penetrated her weary mind. "I . . . I don't think we should sleep together. Carla . . ." She tried to break free of Dan's embrace, but his arms tightened around her like a steel band.

"I told you that's all over. And I told Carla. It's done with, finis, kaput. No more Carla." When her lips parted to speak, he placed his finger over them. "I also told her that when, if ever, I saw her again, it would be in the company of my wife."

"Did you really say that?" Hope and fear surged painfully inside her.

"That's exactly what I said." Dan kissed the corner of her mouth. "I'll help you put the desk in order and lock up. Then we'll go home and have our picnic, Mrs. Welles."

It took only a few minutes for the two of them to roll up the carpets and clear off their individual desks. They stored the ledger and the petty cash box in the safe and put most of the money into the night deposit bag, which they would drop off at the bank on the way home. Then they checked the lock on the front door and activated the alarm system.

Dan led Cassa out to the car, his arm around her waist. "Did I tell you that Laraby, the dog-handler from Apex Alarm System, is using a new type of dog on the premises? It's Belgian—a Bouvier des Flandres. He got it from a breeder who was going to put the animal to sleep because he's a chocolate-brown color with spots. Apparently, spotted Bouviers are considered highly undesirable."

Cassa skidded to an abrupt halt. "You mean the dog would have been killed just for that?" She was incensed.

Dan helped her into the car, his amusement evident. "Don't glare at me, my love. It wasn't my idea. But yes, the dog was definitely going to be destroyed. As I understand it, he's been castrated to prevent him from reproducing his bad genes."

"Ridiculous!" Cassa exploded. "Horrible!"

"Calm yourself, darling." Dan chuckled as he slid into the driver's side, his hand going to her knee. "The animal's fine now. He has a good job as a guard dog earning his keep, and Laraby's very happy with him."

"I should hope so," Cassa said, fuming.

"This is the way you were when we first met, when you were just fifteen—feisty, independent, a defender of the helpless and the homeless." He laughed out loud.

Cassa felt a smile coming. "If you're referring to the dog or two I brought home—"

"Dog or two? I remember three ugly alley cats, one squirrel with no fur on its tail, and at least four lop-eared curs that your father threatened to turn over to the circus."

"But, don't you see?" Cassa exclaimed. "They wouldn't have been abandoned if they'd been good-looking show dogs. The world is filled with pedigreed airheads, both animal and human, who have little to offer except their appearance."

Cassa knew she was overreacting, but she couldn't seem to stop herself. It had been such a long time since she'd felt the idealist's urge to right a wrong. So much of her individuality had been frozen in Suwanon. She'd been unable to think of anything beyond her own survival. But as a young child and later as a teenager, she'd taken up various causes. It was her nature to jump in where angels feared to tread, and worry about the consequences later.

"Do you remember how you used to tell me you were going to stamp out world hunger? And then there was that campaign you planned to wipe out the practice of vivisection," Dan said softly. "In your brave new world there would be no rape, no child- or animal-abuse, no cruelty of any kind."

Cassa nodded. "My big plans went out the window after we married and made Tijanian's our first priority."

"I thought we put each other first," Dan whispered

"We did," she agreed. But to herself she added: Until we began to take each other a little bit for granted. We worked together, we played together; it was a fast, exciting life. But somewhere along the way we lost something, Dan. The pain I felt in Suwanon, the sense of loss, came partly from the realization of all we'd given up, all the beautiful moments we'd sacrificed to the business.

Dan glanced at her, his heart constricting as he noticed how deep in thought, how sad, she looked. Don't think of Suwanon, darling, he urged her silently. Someday I'll tell you what I felt when you were gone from me. How empty my world seemed with just a money-making business and an empty house. I would have given my very life to have been able to kiss you, love you one more time, to tell you that everything had turned to dust because you weren't here to share it with me.

Cassa shook her head to clear it and glanced back at Dan. "I don't mean to sound like a preacher..."

"Preach away, darling," he said lightly. "I love hearing you talk to me about anything."

Cassa stared through the windshield for a moment. "I had lots of time to mull things over in Suwanon, and I came to realize that it isn't the so-called beautiful people who do right in the world. It's the mavericks, the rebels, the out-of-step people who dare to speak up. They're the ones who always get the force for good rolling." Cassa paused, licking her dry lips. "You see, I was alone, and sometimes..." She couldn't tell Dan about the yawning, black loneliness that had assailed her in the deepest night, and sometimes into the daylight hours, too, when she was left by herself in her tiny room. Sometimes they just forgot she was there; they weren't trying to torture her. But that knowledge didn't mitigate the growing, oppressive fear. The tiny walled-in back yard became a haven of light and fresh air, where she could let her mind roam, thinking of anything but her own dire situation. Sometimes she even worked out mathematical theorems in her head—and she had always hated math. She'd entered into imagining dialogs with Schopenhauer, Kafka, and even Voltaire. Her mind and spirit were her salvation.

"You've drifted away again," Dan said gently, jolting her back to the present.

He hid his fear. What was she thinking about? Was she reliving the agonies she'd suffered . . . the rape? His hands whitened on the steering wheel. He cleared his throat. "You were saying that the rebels are the ones who get the force for good moving," he prodded.

"Yes. Then the rest of us jump on the bandwagon." Her voice faltered and faded as Dan, having stopped for a light at Broad Street and Exchange, studied her, his fiery eyes warming her, cosseting her.

"I married a crusader, and I'm glad you're still that way," he said. "I'm glad your experience in Suwanon didn't destroy that part of you. I fully intend to see that my own special girl will never be shut away again." He tried to keep his voice light, though his insides were tied in knots at the thought of her imprisonment. "No one will ever hurt you again," he finished harshly, almost inaudibly.

Hurt her? Cassa was puzzled. What did he mean by that? He must be talking about the accident to her shoulder. She was about to ask when he spoke again, "It's time we both came home . . . to each other. It's time the world backed away and left Dan and Cassa Welles to themselves." He turned the car down the narrow street that led to their house.

As Dan pulled into the short driveway, he said, "I think I'll cut the lawn after we eat. You get to do the trimming."

"Mowing the lawn is the easy job. Trimming and edging are the hard part," Cassa shot back, smiling at him over the roof of the car, pleased by the thought of working around the house with him. It seemed so normal, so ordinary—so safe.

She gazed into the pinkish-purple sky. "I love this place. It really is special. We're in the heart of the city, but here it's as quiet and peaceful as the country." Her nostrils flared as she inhaled the myriad smells of the cool spring evening. "Oh, look at that fool." She pointed to Matt the Cat, who was clambering down the morning glory vines that led from the porch roof to the ground. The cat ambled over to greet them, his tail held high. "I'm sure he'll expect to share our picnic," Cassa said, bending down to stroke their pet.

"Forget it," Dan said as the cat rubbed against his trouser leg. "He's overweight already."

They went inside to change their clothes, sharing a companionable silence. They were just descending the stairs again when the front doorbell chimed.

"Who the hell is that?" Dan grimaced, sprinting down the last two steps to the foyer and opening the door. "Maddy! Hi, honey, come on in," he said, a bit too sweetly.

Maddy rolled her eyes. "I know I'm intruding," she apologized, "but I wanted to bring some of the clothes Gir finished altering."

Dan led the two women into the living room, where he poured a glass of white wine for each of them and for himself. I love you, Maddy, but I sure as hell wish you'd picked another time to visit, he mused silently. He turned his attention to Cassa, running his eyes appreciatively over her peach-colored suit. The outfit gave her eyes a silver sheen and made her hair glisten with blue-black highlights. You are so sexy, my slim, tall darling, so very sexy, Dan thought, admiring her over the rim of his glass.

Dan's reverie was shattered when the doorbell rang again. Dammit. He snapped his teeth together. What did he have to do to get her alone? Sign them up for the next moon launch?

Impatiently, he opened the door to Len, who grinned knowingly. "Am I intruding, Dan?"

"Yes," Dan shot back, unamused when his brother-in-law laughed.

Len walked into the living room ahead of Dan, stopping abruptly when he saw Maddy on the couch. "Hello. I didn't see your car outside." His voice was stiff with surprise.

"It's in the shop. I came by bus." Maddy rose to her feet. "It's a long trip. I should be leaving now."

"Don't go just because I'm here," Len told her.

"I'm not," Maddy replied, bristling.

"Hold it, you two," Dan warned. "You've been married for almost fifteen years—"

"Well, *I* was," Maddy interjected, lifting her chin. "I'm not so sure about Len. His concept of marriage is a little different from mine."

"Maddy," Len said over Cassa's placatory words, "I was unfaithful to you just *once!*"

"You aren't going to start that here," Dan interjected.

Maddy whirled toward the door. "No, we're not. Because I'm leaving."

"I wasn't unfaithful to you with June Stevens or any other woman on that trip to Sacramento. She was in my room alone when she answered the phone because I had sent her there to get the Nelson portfolio." Len glowered at his wife. "But you can believe what you damn well please.If you're ready to leave, I'll drive you home. You're not taking the bus."

Maddy and Len both said good-bye very stiffly and left together. Dan and Cassa stared at one another from across the room.

"I'm glad they're gone," Dan said, coming up to her. "Let's forget them and enjoy our picnic."

"Wait, Dan. Do you think they'll really get a divorce?" Cassa asked, searching his face anxiously.

He hesitated. "Last year I would have said no stronger marriage than theirs existed—except ours, of course. But little by little they're destroying the beautiful relationship they had." He caressed the side of her face. "I don't want that to happen to us."

"Me neither."

Cassa forced all thoughts of Maddy and Len to the fringe of her consciousness, and dinner with Dan was filled with laughter and joy. They drank crisp, tart Genesee cream ale and devoured the white hots, a special Rochester dish. The sliced tomatoes marinated in herb vinaigrette tasted fresh and light. And they finished off the meal with Mrs. Bill's delicious Black Forest cake.

Though they loaded the dishwasher with the silverware and plates, Cassa and Dan elected to do the more delicate crystal by hand rather than save it for the housekeeper, who would arrive at eight the next morning. Cassa found the domestic chore strangely comforting.

Later, she paused in trimming the hedges to watch her T-shirted husband push the hand mower, all that was required for their small yard. He was still the best-looking man she'd ever seen, Cassa decided, taking in the smooth motion of muscles under his shirt, the dampness gathering on his forehead, he looks as if he'd be more at home at the helm of a buccaneer's ship than behind a desk in Tijanian's. She inhaled a shuddering breath. Since the moment she'd first seen him, he'd been all things to her. She'd had a hard time believing that this man who was her sun and moon had wanted to marry her, to stay with her forever.

"Hey, no sloughing off on the job," Dan called to her, grinning as he flipped the mower around, up the drive and into the small shed attached to the two-car garage.

"I'm not sloughing off," Cassa protested. "I just pace myself better than you do."

He came up to her, threw an arm around her neck, and leaned down to place his parted lips over her mouth. His tongue touched hers, withdrew, touched again.

Cassa's insides seemed to turn to dark molasses, thick and sweet. "The neighbors will see," she exclaimed breathlessly.

"Let them get their own girls," Dan retorted, his teeth teasing her bottom lip.

"We could get arrested."

"I know a judge. We'll have him put us under house arrest . . . together," Dan crooned, his eyes dark with desire. But he felt her body stiffen, and the words he'd just spoken echoed in his ears, piercing him with guilt. He held her more tightly against him. "Darling, I'm sorry. That was clumsy. I didn't mean to remind you of your terrible ordeal. I'm so sorry. I don't know why I said that."

"No." Her hands came up to clutch his waist, and she forgot all about the neighbors. "You're right to mention it. We can't pretend those nine months never happened." She looked up at him, feeling the smile falter on her face. "I do want to talk to you about it one day. I want to tell you everything. And I will . . . but a little bit at a time."

She caught her underlip in her teeth. Would Dan still be around when she was ready to talk? Or was he only staying until she settled down and regained some equilibrium? Would he go back to Carla one day?

"Whatever it is that's running around inside your head, making you look so sad, I want you to forget about it now," Dan said sharply. Then his tone softened. "Talk to me instead."

"It's nothing, really." Cassa didn't want to hear him tell

her again that he was through with Carla. It would anger him to think she didn't believe him. She *did* believe him. It was just... She shook her head and put the thoughts behind her.

They crossed the small back yard and entered the enclosed porch where their skis, golf clubs, and tennis equipment was stored.

In the kitchen Dan went to the pantry and brought out a bottle of peach liqueur, which they'd made the summer before. "How about a little celebration before we shower? I worked so hard, I deserve it. And because I'm a sweetheart, I'm going to let you taste, too, even though you didn't work as hard." His eyes glinted at her and his puckish grin widened as she circled around him, her hands flexed into fists. "Wanna wrestle?" he whispered.

"You'd lose." Cassa thrust out her jaw but couldn't contain the laughter bubbling up inside her. Dan had always been able to make her laugh, even when she'd wanted to throttle him.

His arms snaked around her waist and he murmured, "Drink your liqueur, little wife. We're going to take a shower together."

Feeling suddenly shy, Cassa tried to break the mood. "I noticed the new hot tub you had installed, and how you tore down that closet at the end of the hall to make the bathroom larger," she said matter-of-factly.

"I had the workmen start the minute you left for the Middle East," Dan muttered into her neck. "It was to have been your homecoming gift from the buying trip, a surprise." His voice grew hoarse. "It was almost finished when word came that you'd been killed. I don't know when they finished it. I must have paid them. I have the canceled checks, but I don't remember much about that time. I wanted to die with you. I hired people to go to Suwanon to find your body, your possessions, anything that belonged to you. I was told they found your charred passport... and several bodies that were burned beyond recognition." He paused, his eyes haunted, his throat working. "I guess I was pretty hard to get along with for a while."

Cassa wanted to tell him how she'd missed him, how

the image of him in her mind had given her courage and kept her from cracking. But she couldn't! Doubts assailed her. Did he really return her deep, unalterable love? She couldn't test their marriage . . . not yet.

"Cassa, talk to me," Dan urged, his body curved around hers, his arms tightening.

The doorbell rang.

He cursed loudly. He flung the door open and glowered at Denzel Trane, a friendly neighbor who'd always been particularly fond of Cassa.

"Hi, folks." Denzel appeared puzzled when Dan remained in the doorway and made no move to invite him inside. "I just wanted to tell you how happy I am to have you back with us, Cassa. I know you haven't had much time to orient yourself, but I felt I should tell you that there's a community committee meeting at my house tonight. We'll be going over the plans for the Cornhill Festival in July. You and Dan are welcome to come." Denzel bobbed up and down in an effort to see past Dan's arm, which was stretched across the door frame. The Cornhill Festival was an annual neighborhood event. Craftsmen and artisans came from all over the county to sell their wares right there on the streets. Denzel was a true devotee of the fest.

"Thank you, Denzel," Cassa said. "That's very nice of you."

"Sorry, but we have plans this evening," Dan interjected, ushering the man down the steps to the sidewalk. "Have a good evening."

He sprinted back into the house and closed the door behind him with a bang. When Cassa shook her head at him in disapproval, he muttered, "I'll never be alone with you if I let people decide how we spend our time."

"You weren't very friendly." She tried to sound stern but couldn't smother her laughter. "What will he think when he sees our car in the driveway all night?"

"I'll put it in the garage, and then we'll go straight to bed and turn off the lights." Dan squinted out the window at the darkening sky. "It looks like snow anyway."

"Snow? At the end of May? Not even in Rochester." Cassa giggled, feeling cozy and comfortable.

"I'm sure if I looked in the record books I'd find some mention of snow in May," Dan insisted. He locked the door and reached behind him to take her hand and draw her to him. Pointing to the stained-glass window in the door between the foyer and the small entrance hall, he asked, "Remember what I said the first time you brought me here to meet your Uncle Aram?"

"Yes. You said, 'What a beautiful door to lead into a beautiful house. I'd like to live here.'" Cassa smiled up at him, and another of her nameless anxieties melted away.

"Right," Dan murmured, kissing the top of her head before leading her up the curving stairway.

All at once Cassa felt awkward. As they entered their bedroom, her hands felt heavy, her body ungainly. She couldn't look up at Dan, though he kept repeating her name in a soft, coaxing voice.

His hands trembled as he began unbuttoning her blouse. She was so very beautiful! Her face had a luminous glow that made his breath catch in his throat. He had forgotten how long and thick her eyelashes were, how velvety her skin. "Shy with me, darling?" he asked, then had to cough to clear the huskiness from his throat. "I remember how shy you were when we first made love. Shall I confess that I was nervous too?"

Cassa's head snapped up, and she stared at him, mouth agape.

"I knew that would get your attention." Dan chuckled, his fingers caressing her soft skin as he pushed the blouse from her shoulders and threw it into a chair. "I was tense. I didn't want to hurt you. I was afraid you'd be afraid of me."

"I never was," Cassa said breathlessly.

He unzipped her skirt and pushed it down over her hips, then lifted her free of it. "Weren't you, love?" His voice grew unsteady as he unfastened her bra. "Darling, I want to shower before we make love. I'm all sweaty."

"I'd like to shower too." Cassa watched spellbound as he stripped his shirt and jeans from his body and tossed them to the floor. His body should be in the national treasury, she thought. No man should be that beautiful. No human being should have such thick black hair, such brilliant sapphire eyes, such perfectly delineated muscles and long, strong legs.

"I'm perfectly willing to stand here staring at you while you stare at me," Dan whispered, "but as you can plainly see, I'm quite ready to make love to you." His voice touched her like a silken spear, jerking her into awareness and propelling her into the bathroom.

She was acutely aware of Dan right behind her heels as she entered the shower stall and reached for the faucets.

Dan stayed her hand. "Wait. Let's just rinse off quickly, then sit in the hot tub for a few minutes."

Cassa meant to say "No," but her head nodded, and she leaned against him under the shower for a few moments, then let him lead her to the marble hot tub and lift her into the swirling water.

She was deliciously enveloped by the soothing warmth. Then Dan's body was under hers, cushioning it, and she nestled against him. "Isn't this lovely?" he said.

"Yes, I like it."

"Sometimes I hated it." Dan's jaw clenched as he remembered the nights he'd wandered into the room, tormenting himself with memories of her. "This was yours . . . and you weren't here," he said bleakly.

"But I'm here now, Dan." Cassa's body floated away, then back to him. Her hands reached out to touch him, to pull at the wet black hair on his chest, to rub his bristly cheek. She had made no conscious decision to caress him, but her hands seemed to have a will of their own.

"Darling . . ." Dan pulled her hard against him, his body under hers once more, his hands moving restlessly over her moist flesh. "I have to touch you, to make you mine again," he muttered, more to himself than to her.

Willingly she forgot all the uncertainties, left all hesitation behind, as she began to love him fiercely. She clung to his neck, burrowing her face under his chin.

"Dan . . ." Her voice seemed to come from far away. "I was so frightened."

"My baby, my angel . . . Cassa mine," he crooned. "Never, never will I let anyone or anything make you fearful again."

He surged to his feet with Cassa in his arms, then reached for a bathsheet, swathed her in it, and began to pat her dry. When she was still slightly damp he removed the towel and began smoothing lotion all over her body.

"I feel like a houri being prepared to visit her master. Of course I'm not exactly a virgin . . ." Cassa blinked her eyes open and smiled at the sound of Dan's chuckle.

"Nor are you going to be given to anyone in paradise except me." Dan felt his whole body tremble when she wriggled with delight beneath his hands. "Besides, I would be thrown out of paradise for becoming as excited as I am from touching you like this, my lady love."

"I have no complaints," Cassa said happily as he swung her up in his arms and carried her to the bedroom.

He lowered her onto the bed, coming to her side at once. "You're so beautiful, so delicate . . ." His mouth went to her breasts, then slid up to the scar that crossed her shoulder. "So perfect . . ."

Cassa's impatience mounted as he slowly caressed every inch of her body with his mouth. They had always shared an explosive passion, but although Cassa had often told Dan how much she loved him, she had never told him how much she desired him, how she needed him to make love to her. With Dan she had always felt so vulnerable, so open to hurt. She could not verbalize her need, could not admit she wanted him all the time.

Dan lifted his head and gazed deeply into her eyes. "I love you, Cassa."

"I love you, Dan." The words tumbled out of her before she thought to hold them back. "And I want you." As she stared at him, she felt suddenly uneasy, but the blood of passion pumping through her body demanded that she tell him everything. "I want you to make love to me."

"Do you, my angel? I sure as hell want to make love to you. Tell me, tell me what you'd like me to do. I want to please you, make you happy." His face reddened, and his words came out unevenly as he strove to keep himself in check, all the while continuing to stroke her from neck to ankle.

At last his tongue probed gently between her thighs, and

her body arched as warm delight coursed through her. She had never known such mind-bending awe. It felt too perfect to be possible.

Then she was beneath him and he was driving into her with a restrained power that rocked her to the core. All thought dissipated as heightened passion overcame her, until she was matching his every motion, wanting him, giving him all that she was. Her hands were tangled in his hair, his palms were flat on her shoulders and buttocks as they strove to become one in spirit as well as in flesh. Her eyes glazed over with a sensual blindness, nerve ends tingled with a need that was all for Dan, only Dan. When she heard sobbing, she knew it was her own voice calling out to him in ecstasy, even as he groaned against her skin, telegraphing his own satisfaction. Free-falling through love's outer space, they abandoned the world and everyone in it and clung only to each other.

Minutes later Dan lifted his head from her breast. "Oh, my darling. We've made love many times, and it was always good, Cassa, but just now it was beyond anything I've ever experienced."

Unable to speak, Cassa nodded, her eyes filled with tears.

They lay in silence for a while, savoring the precious moments they had just spent together.

Dan insisted they shower together again. Then, refreshed, they went downstairs for a snack of ice-cold milk and oranges. "With you, even the smallest pleasure is an unforgettable event," he murmured, his arm tight around her waist as they ascended the stairs and went back to bed.

Once more Dan loved her, and again Cassa felt the fiery chariot carry her off to a place where he was her only reality.

Later that night, she lay next to Dan, listening to the deep, even breathing that told her he was sound asleep. He lay on his stomach with one arm across her middle and his face close to hers.

She was glad he slept, but sleep eluded her. Not all her skill in blocking out her thoughts helped her this time. Memory took her back to the early years with Dan, before they married, back to when she was nineteen and a sophomore at Rochester Institute of Technology. Dan had graduated from the Wharton School of Business and accepted a job in the marketing division of a large company . . .

One evening in early May, it had been so warm they'd brought the wicker furniture out to the freshly washed porch. Len and Maddy, who had been married the previous December, had invited Dan to dinner at Cassa's parents' home.

Cassa had been coming down the stairs when she'd seen Dan cross the foyer. Until that moment, he had always been Len's friend, indeed, the family's friend. No one knew, she was sure, how she felt about Dan Welles, how she wished she could go out with him, wished that . . .

"Dan, wait!" Cassa had called to him, an idea popping into her mind so suddenly that it made her blink.

He had ambled over to the foot of the stairs and smiled up at her. "What is it, Cassa?"

"Dan, there's a dance at school . . . end of term . . . beer and snacks, and . . . ah, I was wondering if you would like to go with me." She had felt her face turn bright scarlet. Of course he'd say no. She braced herself.

"I'd love to go with you. When is it?"

The roaring in Cassa's ears had blocked out the rest of his words. She didn't even mind when he chuckled and held out a hand to urge her down to his side.

"No matter. We'll work out the details later." And then he had kissed her cheek, making her feel feverish and lightheaded.

The days before the dance had crawled by for Cassa. She made her own dress—a soft sarong of lavender cotton that was both strapless and slimming. Still, she grimaced at herself as she peered into the mirror. "Slim you'll never be, Cassa my girl," she muttered to her reflection. "Not with those hips and that bust." She sighed in resignation.

On the evening of the dance she was again scrutinizing herself in the mirror, toying with a large scarf that matched her dress. After a few minutes' thought, she draped it casually over her shoulders. The weather was warm enough to go without a wrap, but the scarf made her feel more secure: it gave her something to do with her hands . . . and hid some of the fullness of her breasts.

She brushed her short wavy black hair until it shone, and placed lavender lacquered earrings in her pierced ears and a lacquered shell on a gold chain around her neck. Since Dan was so tall, she wore violet sandals with three-inch heels, and she carried a matching clutch purse. The shoes and purse alone had cost her three weeks' wages as a part-time waitress, but she didn't care. It was all for Dan!

As she descended the stairs, he stepped out of the living room with a florist's box in one hand. Even as he smiled at her, he was undoing the wrapping and bringing out one perfect orchid. "Your mother said you could wear it in your hair. There's a comb attached to the flower."

She paused, gulped down her nervousness, and then floated the rest of the way down the stairs to the foyer. Dan led her over to a mirror on the wall and stood behind her as she pinned the flower just over her right ear.

"In the South Pacific when a girl puts a flower over her ear, it means she's ready for marriage," Dan whispered. When she blushed, he chuckled and kissed her cheek. "Of course, I don't know which ear is supposed to have the flower."

"I hope I have it right," she dared to say, and was delighted when he roared with laughter.

She knew she must have said good-bye to her father and mother that evening, but their remarks didn't break the happy spell Dan's presence had cast upon her.

In his car, a classic Thunderbird that he and Len had reconditioned, he had turned to her and grinned. "I think I'm going to like this. Being at the dance with the prettiest girl in the school is every man's dream."

Cassa had known he was teasing her; she knew very well that she was healthy-looking but hardly beautiful. Still she couldn't stop the grin that spread across her face as happiness flooded her whole being. Tonight Dan was hers!

The dance was raucous and fun, the musical group loud and rhythmic. Cassa was delighted to see that, although many of the prettiest and most popular girls tried to catch Dan's eyes, he made it plain that he would be dancing with only her.

They had been circling the room for several minutes when the purple and turquoise lights dimmed and the music changed to a throbbing ballad.

Dan's arms came up to clasp her hip and shoulder as he

pressed her to him. Cassa raised her hands, the eager fingers threading through the crisp black hair at his nape. She took in a deep breath and let it out slowly.

"Do that again, angel," Dan had crooned in her ear. "It feels so damn good. You have heavenly breasts."

Cassa's head snapped back. She stared up at him. Was he making fun of her? She gazed at his half-closed eyes, his sensually slack mouth, and her knees gave way so that she buckled against him.

He held her tighter, taking all of her weight against him. "Cassa, baby, you've grown up at last." He chuckled softly, looking down at her, his penetrating blue stare like a kiss on her mouth. "I love your lips . . . now that you're old enough to be kissed."

Cassa had responded tartly, trying to regain some control of her racing pulse. "I've been kissed many times."

His fingers dug into her body. "Have you? Yes, I suppose at nineteen you must have lots of boyfriends." He muttered the words like a curse.

"Sure," Cassa affirmed, her mouth inches from his. "And you have lots of girl friends."

"Do I?" Dan's mouth came closer. She was planning to tell him to buzz off, but her mouth parted instead. "Your lips are like a dewy flower, Cassa. I like that pearly lipstick. Can I taste it?"

"Yes," she whispered just as his mouth touched hers, lifted, touched again, tasted, lifted. "No," Cassa protested, taking hold of his face and pulling it back down to hers.

Their mouths moved against each other in soft, seductive discovery. And from that moment Cassa was lost. She had always known she loved Dan, but she hadn't known how much. Her fingers clenched in his hair, her body moving invitingly against his. When she felt his throbbing hardness, she was thrilled, not put off the way she had been with the other men she'd dated.

"Really, Cassa, you should get a room," Marian Delby said nastily as she danced by with her date. Marian was popular and sure that anything she did would be approved of and even emulated by all.

Dan lifted his head, but didn't look at Marian. "Cassa, let's get out of here."

They had left the dance hand in hand. Cassa rode home, cuddled as close to Dan as she could get. When she felt his kiss on her hair, she was thrilled and sure he would take her to his apartment. But he hadn't. He had taken her back to her parents' home.

"What's between us is dynamite, angel," he said seriously, rubbing his index finger along her cheek. "And I don't want to spoil it by rushing."

"That won't spoil it," Cassa had urged, pressing her body closer to his.

Dan slid away from her, opened his car door, and came around to her side to help her alight. "It might, and it might not." He kissed her nose as she frowned up at him. "Don't scowl, Cassa. Will you have dinner with me tomorrow night?"

"Yes," she answered at once, a big grin lighting up her face.

He escorted her onto the front porch and pulled her into a dark corner where he took her in his arms again. "I can feel your heart beating through that gorgeous dress. You look like a hot-house flower in it, darling."

"Oh, Dan, don't go," Cassa moaned against his throat.

He kissed her then, his mouth opening on hers, his tongue teasing between her lips, and she felt an electric shock that made her whole body tingle.

She let her body move against his, wanting to be closer, ever closer to him.

Dan thrust her away from him all at once, his breathing harsh and uneven. "Cassa, it's too soon." And not all her persuading could make him stay.

When she entered the house that night, her mother and father were waiting up for her. She stared right through them as if they weren't there, although she did notice their lips moving. Smiling blankly, she floated upstairs to her room without uttering a single word.

The next night she had had dinner with Dan. Afterward their kisses set them on fire. But once again it was Dan who kept a cool head.

Cassa saw him every night for a month.

One evening after they'd had dinner at the Birch Hill Country Club, where both Len and Dan were members, Dan took Cassa back to his apartment.

She was standing in the living room, gazing out the window at Irondequoit Bay when Dan came up behind her and put an arm around her waist. He turned her around to face him and lifted her left hand. "Here." He slipped a beautiful emerald-cut sapphire on her finger and kissed it. "Of course that's only if you, and your father, approve."

Cassa threw herself into his arms, and this time when he would have pushed her away, she refused to let him. Triumph and delight filled her to overflowing as Dan carried her into his bedroom and slowly removed her clothes.

"Darling, I shouldn't. You're a virgin. You should have your wedding night," he muttered, his mouth on her breast.

"*This* is my wedding night. I love you, Dan."

The pain she had been led to expect was nothing compared to the dizzying heights she scaled with Dan. She had never imagined such an explosion of feeling, both gentle and wrenching, fearsome and sweet.

They were married three months later. Cassa was radiant in a white silk Empire-style gown she had made herself, and Dan looked resplendent in his morning suit. Maddy and Len were their only attendants.

5

ON THE DAY of the country club benefit dance in late June, about a month after Cassa's return, she was waiting on a customer at the store and wishing she didn't have to attend it. She had been friendly with some people at the club, but most could be considered only acquaintances, and the thought of spending hours drinking and listening to dull stories about golf games and tennis matches was thoroughly unappealing. Once she'd delighted in bantering over cocktails; now the very idea bored her. If the dance weren't being held to raise money for charity, she would have found some reason to beg off. At least Maddy and Girardot would be going with them.

"Pardon me," said Cassa's customer, interrupting her musings. "What were you saying about the knots in this Sarouk?"

Cassa took a deep breath, smiled at the woman and began pointing out how the density of knots and the vibrant reds and jewel-toned blues gave the carpet its luxurious appearance. "Though it's a secondhand rug, it's still in fine condition. The colors stand up against even the newer carpets.

As you can see, even down on our hands and knees as we are, there's no noticeable wear." Cassa rose and helped the woman to her feet. "Mrs. Gladston, this is a very good buy, and even if you decide to sell it in a year or two, you'll probably get what you paid for the rug in trade on another carpet."

Cassa nodded to three other people who had just entered the store. The business was thriving. Oriental rugs were enjoying a resurgence of popularity after several years in which wall-to-wall carpeting had been in vogue. To Cassa, wall-to-wall carpeting was a shoddy, unattractive way to cover a floor. She would always prefer hardwood floors and fine orientals.

She was happy to close up shop at noon, which was their custom on Saturdays, and join Dendor and Dan in the back room. "Can I help log the receipts?" she asked brightly.

Dan was just hanging up the phone, but he smiled and gestured to her to sit down beside him. "That was Max at the Syracuse store. They've just closed a big order with the museum down there." He watched her lean over the ledger. "Don't worry about that, darling. Dendor has just about finished the logging."

"And Armand, my friend, is joining me for lunch at one o'clock at the University Club, so I will be glad to close the store," the old Armenian offered.

Dan patted his lap. "Or we can stay, and you can sit here and help me."

Dendor snorted as Cassa sniffed and shook her head. "Do not *ask* her, Danilo," he said. "Tell her she is to cuddle with you on your lap."

"Dendor!" Cassa glared, trying to mask her amusement.

Dendor looked at Dan. "I can see that deep down she is smiling, Danilo."

Dan jumped up from his chair and whisked Cassa into his arms, whirling her around him. "Yes, I can see it too." And right in front of Dendor, he kissed her, his mouth savoring hers, his heart hammering in his chest at the feel of her.

"Dan!" Cassa gasped, her lips mere centimeters from his.

"That's how a true Armenian handles a woman," Dendor said, nodding in approval. "He loves her to death."

"Proper punishment," Dan muttered, letting her slide down his body but not taking his eyes off her. "We'll see you Monday, Dendor, my friend."

"In truth, you will Danilo." Dendor rose from his chair and kissed Cassa on the cheek. "Behave yourself, or you shall have more punishment."

"Dendor, you are a sexist," Cassa accused breathlessly, as she and Dan left the store.

Dan led her by the hand to the car, which was parked in the alley. "Guess where we're going two weeks from Tuesday?" He eased her into the passenger side and closed the door, then slipped into the driver's seat and leaned over to kiss her nose.

"To work?" Cassa felt weak with happiness because Dan was so close to her.

"Wrong. I'm going to take you to Darien Lake, the amusement park near Medina."

"An amusement park?" Cassa was stunned. "You'll hate it."

"Wrong again." Dan wheeled the car across the Broad Street Bridge toward Plymouth Avenue, which would take them to Cornhill. "They advertise the biggest Ferris wheel in the state and a roller coaster that makes complete circles."

"You'll lose your lunch." Cassa giggled, arranging her knees beneath her on the seat and leaning toward him.

Dan's hand left the wheel to grasp her thigh. "Me? Iron Man Welles? How you talk, wife of mine. I intend to set a new endurance record for roller-coaster riding." He thumped himself on the chest.

Cassa laughed out loud, feeling light as air.

Dan pulled into their narrow street and parked in front of the house. He shut off the engine and turned to her. "When you were gone, I wanted to hear that sound more than I've ever wanted anything."

"What sound?" Once again and without any warning, Cassa felt shy with him.

"Your laughter, your giggles, your chuckles—all your happy sounds that haunted me when I thought you were gone." A spasm ran like forked lightning up Dan's cheek.

"I thought of you every day." Mentally Cassa amended that: I thought of you every moment, Daniel Casemore Welles.

"I never want you to stop thinking of me, angel." Dan came around to her side of the car, helped her out, and put his arm around her waist. "I called Maddy and Gir today and invited them over for cocktails before the dance. I thought it would be more intimate. Okay?"

"Yes." Cassa was relieved that they'd be starting the evening at home with friends before braving the chaos of the club.

"Your brother may be joining us, too, Cassa."

"I didn't know that."

"When I talked to him a couple of days ago, he said that when he took Maddy home from our house the night after you returned, they'd talked more than they had in a long time." Dan shrugged. "But, then again, he might *not* come, so I haven't said anything to Maddy."

Cassa nodded.

"I asked Mrs. Bills to make some canapes. That should hold us until we have dinner at the club," Dan said as they went inside and up to their room to change.

Cassa took a quick shower and shampoo, then stood under the light in the bathroom to dry her long black hair. As she stared at herself in the full-length mirror on the back of the bathroom door, she noted that she looked a lot longer and leaner than she had before going to Suwanon. Even her feet were narrower. She'd always been tall, but now she looked willowy. She held her heavy hair off her neck and frowned. "I have to get it cut," she said aloud.

"Please, don't cut it." She turned to find Dan in the doorway wearing nothing but his undershorts. "It's perfect, like a black waterfall, so thick and silky. Please keep it that way for me, just for a while."

Cassa opened her mouth to explain how long it took to dry and style her hair when it was this length, but seeing his intense expression, she softened. "All right, I'll keep it this way . . . for now."

"Thank you, darling." Dan straightened away from the

door jamb and came forward to kiss her shoulder. "Maybe we should call our guests and tell them not to come, that we won't be going," he mumbled, his hands tracing slow circles over her derriere.

"Dan, we can't." Cassa sighed dreamily as she swayed toward him. Her head was settling comfortably on his shoulder, but as he reached up to stroke her hair, she caught a glimpse of his wristwatch. "Oh dear," she cried, pushing away from him, inch by inch. "Our guests will be here in less than an hour."

His hand feathered her spine, down and up again, then lingered on her buttocks. Lord, how he loved her body. Too slender or not, she was breathtaking to him. It took all his control not to pick her up in his arms, place her on the bed, and let their passions transport them to another world.

Alone in their bedroom while Dan was showering, Cassa took deep breaths to steady herself. Lord, he was lethal. His mere touch could reduce her to a panting teenager. She squeezed her eyes tightly shut. The special tingling she had felt since her first meeting with Dan had not faded with the years. Instead, it had grown, swelled, burgeoned.

Shaking her head to clear it of Dan, she donned a silky wraparound robe that he had given her one Christmas and sat down to apply her makeup.

Before her trip to the Middle East, she had used makeup sparingly, often finding it tiresome to powder and paint. But since her imprisonment, when she'd been denied even the most basic amenities, she had delighted in what Maddy called "daubing on the war paint."

As she applied pale gold eye shadow to her lids, she considered the dress she'd be wearing that evening. Maddy had dropped it off at Tijanian's the previous day.

"Girardot says this will be perfect for you," she'd said. "It will cover your shoulder scar . . . not that I think you should worry about such things. Everyone knows what you've been through." When Cassa opened her mouth to speak, she held up a hand, palm outward. "I know, I know. It bothers you to talk about it. I do understand how you feel." Maddy handed her the box. "This will cover you . . . ostensibly." Her sister-in-law gave her a sly smile, waved good-bye, and was gone before Cassa could question her.

"What have Gir and Maddy gotten me into?" Cassa now asked out loud. She had looked at the dress last night and decided she liked the pale orange color, but the sheer material had her worried.

After adding a final dab of pale orange lip gloss, she rose from the dressing-table stool. Her hair was swept back from her forehead and fell in soft waves down her back. She clipped it in place with diamond-and-gold pins that had belonged to Uncle Aram's wife, Melissa.

She got into the champagne-colored body stocking, delighting in its lightness and comfort. Then she put on the gossamer silk caftan that Gir thought would be so perfect on her. It had a round neckline and mid-length bishop sleeves. Barefoot Cassa twirled in front of the mirror, then exclaimed, "Good Lord, it's so sheer I look almost naked."

She slipped into a pair of low-heeled sandals and glanced at the clock on the nightstand. Gir and Maddy would be arriving any minute now. She called to Dan that she was going downstairs, but didn't quite catch his muffled response.

She had been downstairs for a few minutes, placing trays of canapes on the round rosewood table in front of the fireplace, when she heard a gasp behind her. She straightened up and found Maddy staring at her.

"We just walked in. The door was open," Girardot explained jauntily. Grinning broadly, he glanced from Cassa to a still-agape Maddy. "Didn't I tell you she'd look sensational in that outfit?"

"It's outrageous!" Maddy cried, putting a hand on Cassa's arm. "Oh, Cass, darling, I don't mean you're outrageous. You look like a goddess in that caftan. You're so sylphlike, so . . . so sensual," Maddy enthused, circling her slowly. "You're one gorgeous lady. It's a wonder Dan even let you out of the bedroom."

"Don't be ridiculous." Gir glared at Maddy. "The little number you're wearing is just as revealing." He looked down his thin nose at the strapless sarong of steel-blue silk that Maddy had swatched around her tiny but well-developed frame.

Maddy blushed and Cassa laughed.

"Has the party begun without me?" Dan asked, ambling into the room, a jeweler's box in his hand. "Gir. Hello, Maddy, darlin'." He greeted Gir with a handshake, Maddy with a kiss.

Then he turned to Cassa, who had just finished pouring drinks for their guests. "I wanted you to wait for me—" His voice halted abruptly as his wife moved toward Maddy and Gir, a glass in each hand. "Cassa!" he gasped.

"Gin and lime for you, Maddy. Rum and branch water for you, Gir," Cassa offered, trying to ignore her husband's outraged expression. "Can I get something for you, Dan?"

"I'll have a beer," he muttered, still staring at her.

"I can see you like my 'Temptation' creation, Dan," Gir said proudly, taking a swallow of his drink and smacking his lips."I knew it was just the thing for Cassa's tall, lissome frame."

"Did you?" Dan growled menacingly, swinging around to face the other man, his hands balled into fists at his sides.

"Here's your beer, Dan. Icy cold," Cassa said, stepping neatly between the two men.

Glowering at both Gir and Cassa, Dan accepted the beer and thrust the jewelry box into her hands. "Here. Something for you to wear. Not that anybody will notice with you in that dress." He scowled at her as she snapped open the lid and stared at the white jade pin and earrings nestled against the deep blue velvet.

"Dan, thank you! They're so lovely," Cassa said softly, reaching up to kiss him on the mouth.

"Of course you can't wear them tonight. That dress requires no additional adornment," Gir pronounced, going to the antique rosewood sideboard, which Cassa and Dan had refinished as a bar, and pouring himself another drink.

Cassa glared at him. "Keep your opinions to yourself, Gir. I'm wearing the jade. I love it." Cassa went to the gilt-framed mirror above the fireplace and affixed the earrings and pin. Just then the doorbell rang. Her eyes met Dan's in the mirror. Len?

Dan shrugged and turned to Gir. "Get the door, will you?" he said coolly. Damn Girardot, he thought, designing that beautiful dress for Cassa. And damn me for being so jealous. What the hell is the matter with me? I feel off-balance all the time where she's concerned. He watched her in the mirror, heat coursing through his body as his eyes roved slowly over her. "You're too beautiful to take anywhere," he whispered in her ear. "Let's stay home and tell Gir to take my car."

"Well, look who's here!" Gir called from the doorway. Everyone's head turned.

"Good evening," Len said, coming across the room to kiss his sister on the cheek and shake Dan's hand. Then he stood stock still, staring down at Maddy, who was sitting stiffly on the settee in front of the Adams fireplace. Her drink was poised halfway to her mouth. All the color had drained from her face. "Hello, Maddy," Len said softly.

"Hello, Len." Maddy gulped down a too-big swallow of gin and began to cough.

Cassa patted her on the back. "Well, it's good to see you," she said with feigned brightness, hurrying across the room to her brother. "We weren't sure you'd be joining us." She smiled weakly and glanced sideways at Maddy.

"I know. When Dan mentioned that you were all going with him, it occurred to me that you might be a little bit cramped in either Gir's car or Dan's. So I brought the Caddy."

"Great," Dan said, pounding his brother-in-law on the back, then offering him a beer. When Len nodded, the two men walked to the bar, where they were joined by Girardot.

Cassa looked down at her sister-in-law. "Dan told me this evening that Len might come," she said sotto voce, "but I wasn't sure he would. Do you mind him being here?"

Maddy sighed. "We had quite a talk the last time we met. We were like two geysers erupting. I realize now that I could have been wrong about Len's actions." She gave Cassa a half-smile. "Divorce is a damned final step to take. I think we should try harder to work things out before we part company for good."

"Oh, Maddy, I hope you can. I hate the thought of you and Len being divorced," Cassa admitted.

Maddy was about to reply when Gir ambled over to them.

"Isn't it great that we'll be riding in comfort instead of being bounced black and blue in my heap or crushed to death in Dan's sports car." He chuckled.

"Dan's car has plenty of room," Cassa said, watching Maddy. Her sister-in-law's eyes had gone to Len, who was leaning against the bar talking to Dan.

"Don't be an ass, Cass," Gir went on. "Hey, that's poetry, by God. I'm so talented!"

"You're the ass," Cassa snapped.

"What does that mean?" Gir glared at her, then glanced at Maddy, who was biting her lower lip. "Sorry, I didn't think. Will this make you uncomfortable, Madeleine?"

Just then Dan set his glass down with a clink. "Time to go. Leave these things, Cassa. We'll clean up when we get home."

Before Cassa could formulate a protest, Dan was at her side, guiding her up from the settee, then reaching down for Maddy. They hardly had time to set down their drinks. "Let's go. You women get to sit in the back seat. All I ask is that you fight over me."

"You fool," Maddy said affectionately, smiling up at him and visibly relaxing.

The ride to the club wasn't nearly the torture Cassa had anticipated. Dan asked Gir one question about his new line of clothes, due out the following spring, and the conversation proceeded without pause for the entire trip.

But when Len brought the large, sleek car up the drive, Cassa felt numb with anxiety. She licked her suddenly dry lips and reminded herself that she and Dan had spent many happy hours at the club. But she couldn't stifle a growing fear of the crowded, smoke-filled rooms, of people pressing close against her, firing questions at her about her imprisonment. Already she felt the pressure mounting, as the interior of the car seemed to close in on her. She shivered, and moisture beaded her upper lip.

Dan leaned closer, his eyes concerned. "Are you cold, angel? Let me put my jacket around you."

"I'm not cold. I just . . . I feel . . ." She couldn't verbalize her vague anxiety. She hadn't experienced even a hint of claustrophobia at home, or in their store, or even at the mall. Why was she feeling so uneasy here? She skated around the truth by saying, "It seems like a lifetime ago since I was here. It feels strange."

"Damn!" Dan's jaw clenched, and he ran a restless hand

through hair hair. "I should have driven us separately. Then we could go home whenever we chose."

"Yes, that would have been nice," Cassa agreed.

"Don't worry, darling. I'll take care of you." He slipped an arm around her.

"Are you two getting out?" Gir asked. He and Maddy were standing on the pavement beside the Caddy.

"We're coming," Dan replied tersely, sliding across the seat and helping Cassa from the car.

The four of them moved slowly toward the front entrance, which was festooned with gaily colored lights. Len told the valet exactly where to park his car.

"He always does that," Maddy complained.

As Len joined them, they passed through the front door and were at once accosted by an acquaintance of Len's. When the rest of them began moving toward the banquet room, where the party was in full swing, Len caught Maddy's arm. "You know Doug, don't you, Maddy?"

Maddy looked back at Cassa, who would have stopped too, but Dan said firmly, "Not that way, this way, Cassa. Len and Maddy know the man."

"Yes, but Maddy . . ."

Ignoring his wife's protest, Dan led her into the flower-bedecked glass-walled room that club members called the Lanai.

A large woman approached them. "Cassa! How are you? Remember me? Lorinne Grady." The mahogany-skinned platinum blonde planted herself in front of Cassa, her brown-and-green striped taffeta gown emphasizing the sallowness of her complexion.

"Of course I remember you." Cassa stepped slightly back from the woman, whose smile seemed to have stretched into grotesque proportions. It comforted Cassa to feel Dan at her back, one hand massaging her waist, his breath gently stirring her hair.

"Well, I wasn't sure." Lorinne exhaled a stream of cigarette smoke straight at Cassa. "Carla said you were in such a bad way."

"Bull," Girardot said emphatically, his body taut with anger. "Cassa is fine. And she has more levelheadedness and common sense, not to mention clothes sense, than anyone I know."

"That's for sure." Dan laughed, hugging his wife closer and kissing her cheek. He smiled at Lorinne Grady with cool politeness, then said, "Would you excuse us? We'd like to get a drink."

Gir gave the taffeta dress a disdainful look and added, "Yes, please do excuse us. I really need a drink."

As they continued to the bar, nodding and smiling at acquaintances, Cassa scolded Gir. "She turned so red."

"Well, she *should* have been embarrassed, wearing that hideous . . . awning. I cannot call it a gown." He looked thoughtful. "I think she stole it from Eddie's Pub. I'm sure they had one just like it over the front door." Haughtily, Gir looked down his nose before smiling at Dan, who was gesturing toward the bar. "Thanks. Rum and branch water would be fine." Then, turning his attention back to Cassa, he muttered, "When will women with hips like swinging doors stop wearing fabrics that are fit only for hot-air balloons?"

"I have . . . I had big hips," Cassa ventured, feeling safe and secure with Dan and Gir beside her.

"Yes, you did, my little pumpkin, but with your height and style, your graceful, athletic walk, you never looked like a tugboat charging full steam ahead." Gir pursed his lips, studying her as though she were a plaster mannequin he was dressing. "Of course, you really shouldn't have worn the jade, but . . ." He hurried on as Cassa began to protest. "Now, with your new sylphlike figure—as Maddy so aptly put it—you have even more panache. You are without a doubt the most glamorous woman in this room." Teasingly, Cassa preened, and he snorted, "For goodness sake, don't act like a peahen just because I complimented you, Cassa. Though of course my approval is all anyone needs to be considered well dressed in this town."

"I am not a peahen," she sputtered indignantly. "You conceited—"

"Preen like a peahen if you wish, my gorgeous orange bird of paradise," Dan murmured, lowering his head to nibble at her ear. "You're so lovely."

A sunburned man came up to them, his hand outstretched, his paunch somewhat disguised by the excellent cut of his dark suit. Cassa recognized him as Charles Marvin, one of Dan's frequent golf partners. "Hello, Cassa. Welcome home. Are you going to save a dance for me?"

"Hello, Charles. How are you?" Several other people joined them as she and Charles embraced. They all started speaking at once, and ten right hands were held out to be shaken. Cassa's head began to pound.

With increasing anxiety she realized that Dan and Gir had wandered quite a way off from her. Her palms grew damp, her knees felt suddenly weak, and her throat tightened. She tried to keep calm and cool and to reply appropriately to the guests' bantering comments, but the individual people had become a sea of faces with open mouths—laughing, talking, questioning.

Her ears roared, her eyes blurred, her heart raced. Moisture formed on her forehead and upper lip. Suddenly she could hardly breathe!

When a powerful arm slipped around her waist, she was startled almost out of her wits.

"Easy, angel," Dan murmured soothingly. "I thought you might need me." He smiled down at her, trying to mask his concern. He'd glimpsed the panic in her eyes, and he was sure she was remembering those terrible months in Suwanon. Was she reliving the assault? His stomach churned painfully as he imagined the tortures she'd endured, the nightmare she was mentally reliving now. Damn them all to the hottest fires of hell! He struggled not to let his inner turmoil show through his smile. He had to protect her!

"I did need you." Her lips trembled as the claustrophobic feeling receded. "I *do* need you." Her shaky laugh faded away as their eyes locked in intimate communication.

A woman's voice broke the spell between them. "What's it like to come back and find your husband engaged to marry a beautiful woman?" Cassa turned to see Nancy Jones, a long-time friend of Carla's, at her elbow.

Silence fell in a circle around them as everyone within hearing distance strained to hear Cassa's reply.

She took a deep breath. "That's a very rude question,

Nancy. Why would a supposedly intelligent woman ask it?" She lifted her chin proudly.

"Atta girl, Cassa," Maddy said at her side, glaring up at Nancy, her diminutive figure quivering in outrage. To Nancy she said, "Dan Welles thought his wife was dead. He was willing to settle for Carla in a misguided attempt to forget his grief."

Nancy's eyebrows rose, and she exhaled twin streams of smoke through her nose. "Really?"

"Yes, really." Though Maddy wasn't smoking, Cassa imagined she saw smoke coming out of her loyal sister-in-law. Maddy's such a fighter, she thought affectionately.

Cassa heard a smattering of appreciative laughter as Maddy took a deep breath before going on, but Len suddenly appeared and put his arm around her waist, edging her away.

"Come on, my little tiger. Gir has saved us a table, and it's time to eat. Your little lamb"—he chuckled as Maddy struggled against him for a moment—"has no further need of her protective mama."

"Well, I certainly wasn't going to stand there and let that . . . that woman insult Cass. I should have socked her in the eye," Maddy fumed, as both Dan and Len laughed. Cassa gave her beloved defender a watery smile.

"Mad, my love, I have often said I should use you to defend my clients. You'd win the jury over every time." Len escorted her to a chair, then sat down beside her, one arm along the back of the seat, his body bent toward her.

"Don't call me Mad," Maddy said testily as she stared up into his eyes.

"I would really like to eat, if you battling Amazons would call a halt to your bellicose remarks for a short while," Gir said, staring moodily at Maddy and Cassa.

"You mushroom," Maddy retorted.

Gir leveled her with his most quelling look. "Mushroom, am I? Listen to me, Madeleine Louise Tellier—"

"Davis," Len interjected, thrusting his menu at the attendant and proceeding to trim a slim cheroot with a gold knife. "She's still married to me."

"You shouldn't smoke those things, especially before you eat," Maddy said, two spots of color high on her cheeks.

"Stay married to me, and I promise I won't touch another," Len replied, fixing his eyes on her.

No one spoke. The tension at the table grew. The waiter's arrival with a bottle of chilled wine brought a welcome relief.

"My goodness, the music has begun already," Cassa said nervously, clearing her throat.

"Yes, even before the fruit cup," Gir observed sarcastically, rolling his eyes.

"Darling." Dan leaned toward Cassa, unable to hold back the question that had filled his thoughts ever since she'd panicked in the crowded room. He didn't want to revive painful memories, but if she didn't talk about it, she might never get over her traumatic experience. "Love," he said softly, massaging her neck with gentle fingers. "Tell me what happened before. What were you thinking about? It scares me to see you look so frightened." His mouth grazed her cheek.

Despite his caresses, her anxiety returned. "The crowds of people . . . they seemed to close in," Cassa tried to explain, hysteria rising in her voice. She pressed her lips together and shook her head, unable to go on.

"I understand," Dan said, but inside he was cursing himself. Of course she didn't want to discuss it, sitting there at the table. His timing was abominable. He had been stupid to say anything. "I tried to reach you as fast as I could," he said finally.

"I know. Thank you." Cassa turned grateful eyes to his and was surprised by the flash of emotion she saw on his face. His nostrils flared, and he inhaled sharply.

"Love, when you look at me like that, I feel as if I could go out and conquer Persia."

"Iran," Cassa corrected.

"What?" Dan leaned toward her, their noses almost touching.

"Persia is the ancient name of Iran," Cassa explained, giddy from his nearness.

"I know." Dan chuckled and kissed the corner of her mouth. "Shall we try Mesopotamia?" His teeth fastened on her lower lip.

"It's now Iraq mostly," Cassa managed to say. Her eyes slid closed as his kiss sent languid warmth coursing through her veins.

"You ordered the sole amandine, madam?" The waiter leaning over Cassa earned a glare from Dan and a chuckle from Len.

"Huh?" Cassa stared at the sizzling plate of aromatic fish. "Looks good," she said weakly.

"I ordered the same," Dan snapped.

Though not gourmet fare, the meal was tasty, and Cassa could find no fault with anything as long as Dan's thigh was pressed against hers and he could reach for her hand, which he did often. As they finished up with cheese, fruit, and coffee, Cassa was convinced she had just eaten the best meal of her life—or was that just because Dan was with her?

To much applause, several people stood up to report on the monies collected for the group homes in the county. The audience cheered and laughed. The benefit dance was a great success.

Afterward, Cassa and Maddy retired to the powder room. Cassa was applying lip gloss when she glanced over at Maddy, who was frowning into the mirror. "What's wrong? Do you feel uncomfortable with Len here?"

"No." Maddy shook her head. "The problem is that I don't. It always feels right with Len. But we've been separated for a while, and I don't know what to do next. I want to believe what Len tells me, but I'm afraid. After I learned he'd been unfaithful to me, I just didn't feel I could trust him again. He'd broken a major bond in our marriage."

Cassa squeezed Maddy's hand in sympathy. "It's true Len has a flirtatious nature, but he does love you, Maddy. I'm sure of it."

"I've seen the way women look at him, the way he assesses them in return." Maddy bit her lip.

"Dan does that too." Cassa gave her sister-in-law a wry smile. "Being married to an attractive man ain't easy." Her smile faded as she added, "But when I was in Suwanon, I realized that Dan is the center of my life, my very reason for being. Without him, I would be only half alive. It may sound silly, but I feel that, without him, I wouldn't be able to see as clearly, my hearing would not be as sharp, my other senses would be dull, numb." She stared at Maddy. "In Suwanon I decided that if I ever made it home, back to Dan, I would work hard to make our lives even better than before. I'd make sure we had more time for each other." She felt her smile tremble. "I wouldn't sweat the small stuff—as Len used to say; and I wouldn't get upset over little things." Cassa looked down at her hands. "Just staying alive was such a challenge over there, yet I knew then that if I didn't have Dan in my life, living would be mere existence, just breathing in and out. All the joy would be gone, the exhilaration, the delight I feel just in opening up my eyes each day." Cassa swallowed hard. "I can't tell you what to do with your life, Maddy. I can only tell you that in Suwanon I made up my mind to fight for my life—because of Dan." She looked back into the mirror, lifting a shaking hand to push back a strand of hair.

Maddy hugged her warmly. "Heavy stuff, baby sister." Maddy's voice threatened to break as she used her special nickname for Cassa. "It would be hell not to see Len again." Her eyes shone with unshed tears. "But I wonder if Len and I are strong enough to forget the past and allow ourselves to trust each other again?"

"Only you two can answer that question. But I did learn in Suwanon that we all have more strength than we sometimes suppose we do."

"Do you think I'm wrong to be living apart from Len, Cassa?"

"I can't answer that, either, but I want you to know I'll still be your friend whatever you decide."

The two women left the powder room and made their way through the crowd around the bar. Several couples were gyrating on the dance floor. Conspicuous among them was Girardot, who was doing an original if somewhat out of step tango with an older woman who seemed to be enjoying herself despite her eccentric partner's antics.

Watching them, Maddy and Cassa giggled merrily.

"Shame on you two, laughing at poor Gir," Len said at their side. "Dan has a table for us in the other room. Ah, the music is changing." He looked down at his wife. "Maddy, would you like to dance?"

"No . . . I . . ." She looked at Cassa who smiled encouragingly.

Len inclined his head and gazed out at the dance floor, his mouth a tight line.

Maddy put a hesitant hand on his arm and said softly, "I . . . I think I *would* like to dance." Her eyes asked for understanding. "If the offer is still open."

Len stared down at her, then up at her face. "The offer is still open," he answered huskily, his eyes lighting up as he slipped an arm around her slim waist and led her to the floor.

"Don't mind me. Of course, you're excused," Cassa called after them sarcastically as they walked away without a backward glance.

"Have you been abandoned?" asked a good-looking man at Cassa's side. It was Telford Jones, Nancy's brother. His blond hair was sun-streaked and his skin darkly tanned.

"Not really," Cassa replied. She had always found Tel to be an amiable man.

"Well, I have. Been abandoned, I mean." He put his drink down on a nearby table and held out his arms. "Take pity on a lonely man and dance with me."

Cassa hesitated momentarily before nodding. "All right."

Tel caught her around the waist with surprisingly strong arms and whirled her around the good-sized dance floor to the big-band sound of the song "String of Pearls." Her long, lissome body took on a new lightness as the rhythm seemed to enter her being and bubble through her veins. A carefree, almost giddy feeling overtook her, and she let herself go as Tel Jones skillfully directed her movements in time to the powerful beat of the music.

As she became aware that some of the other dancers had stopped to watch them, Cassa's steps momentarily faltered, but when she would have stopped dancing altogether, Tel caught her to him again and turned and dipped her in perfect time.

They finished out the song to much laughter and clapping. But Cassa's smile faded as she saw Dan pushing his way through the throng, Carla at his heels.

"Darling, do let her dance," the other woman sang out as the slow music began again. "I want to dance too."

"Good," Dan said tensely. "Jones, Carla wants to dance with you. I'll take my wife now."

Cassa felt herself pulled away from Tel Jones and into Dan's powerful arms. She braced herself for the angry words she knew were coming. But he kissed her ear and held her close instead. "I'm wildly jealous of him, Cassa," he admitted seriously. "You looked so good out there. Your movements were so sensual, so lovely." He punctuated the words with tiny bites on her neck that sent shiver after shiver down her spine.

"Dan," she cried softly, clasping her hands around his neck.

"I wanted to be the first one to dance with you after your return. I wanted it," he muttered into her neck. "I could have broken his jaw for dancing with you."

"Dan! You can't mean that," she gasped. He had always been so cool, so calm, so unflappable.

"Let him come near you again tonight, and we'll see, won't we?" he whispered, his lips tasting the corner of her mouth.

"You're being silly." Cassa inhaled sharply as he cradled her even closer, his body moving against hers in a sensual appeal. "Dan, we'll be asked to leave." She gasped again, then laughed as he molded his body to hers.

"Yes, let's leave," he mumbled.

Cassa's eyes closed in rapture, then opened wide. "We didn't bring the car," she reminded him.

"I'll call a taxi."

As she was about to nod yes, Cassa noticed Maddy dancing with Gir, but looking over his shoulder at Len, who was now tangoing with Nancy Jones. Len threw his head back as he laughed at something she said. "Dan, we can't leave yet. Maddy and Len—"

"Will have to solve their own problems," he finished for her. "If they're stupid enough to let pride keep them apart, then they've earned the hell they'll be occupying." Dan's face was taut with disapproval. "I know what it feels like to lose someone you love, but I can't tell Maddy and Len how to behave."

As their bodies continued to sway to the music, Cassa looked up at the beloved face above her. "Dan, I want to go home with you, but Maddy is my friend. Len is my brother."

"They don't need you much as I do." But he nodded resignedly, his chin resting on her head. "We'll stay." He led her back to the table, one arm tight around her waist.

Maddy and Gir returned at almost the same moment.

"Madeleine, my sweet, dance with me." Dan smiled down at his sister-in-law, pulling her out of her chair with the same motion he'd used to seat Cassa in hers.

"What a cave man you are, Daniel Welles," Maddy said, a sweet smile illuminating her pale face.

When Len returned to the table, Gir and Cassa were discussing the merits of the other dresses in her new wardrobe.

"Excuse me, Girardot," Cassa said. "Come on, Len, let's dance." She rose to her feet and held out her arms to him, even as she spotted Nancy Jones crossing the floor and heading straight for their table.

"Right." Len's eyes slid to the corner of the room where Maddy and Dan were doing an energetic—and undefinable—dance. "Don't expect me to be as good at this as Dan is."

"I don't," Cassa answered sweetly, dancing around her brother, grinning when he grimaced at her. "I don't blame Maddy for staying separated from you."

Len jerked her toward him. "What do you mean by that?" he demanded.

"Keep dancing, brother mine," Cassa caroled, breaking free of him and moving freely to the beat of the music. "What I meant was"—she didn't lose a step as she stared into his eyes—"that you seem to be doing everything in your power to convince Maddy that you've been unfaithful to her. Wait a minute." Cassa waved a hand imperiously when he began to protest. "I haven't finished."

"Well, I've heard enough."

"All right, lose her. Is that what you want?"

"No, damn you, Cassa. It's not what I want."

"Then listen to some good advice, brother. You can't continue to flirt with all the women you see—"

"I don't!"

"—dancing with them, complimenting them, and still convince Maddy that you want her back, that other women don't interest you."

"They don't."

"Then stop being a fool and mount a campaign to win her back. Make sure she knows she's the only woman you want."

"She is." Len stopped dancing and gazed across the floor to see a laughing Maddy collapse into Dan's arms as the music changed to a slower tempo. "Come on." Pulling his sister after him, he threaded his way past the dancing throng and tapped Dan on the shoulder. "I've brought you your wife. I'd like mine back." Len ignored Maddy's gasp of surprise and drew her to him. "I'll be your only partner for the rest of the night," he declared.

"Go get 'em, tiger." Cassa waved at a slack-jawed Maddy who was being held tight against Len's lean body.

"Do gooder," Dan whispered.

Cassa was smiling into his eyes when Carla swept up to them, Tel Jones at her side.

"I was saying to Tel that you promised me a dance, and he said that he'd love to dance with Cassa." Carla beamed.

"Dan was just going to get a taxi." The words seemed to slip from Cassa's mouth.

Dan glanced down at her with approval. "So I was." He turned back to the other couple. "Another time perhaps." And without another word, he led Cassa from the floor, his arm around her waist. "Let's hurry, angel."

6

A WEEK LATER Dan arranged for them to take another day off to go to Darien Lake. "But we can't keep asking Dendor to mind the store," Cassa protested.

"Why? He loves it." Dan grinned and nudged her into the bathroom. "You take your shower first. I'm going downstairs to make sure Mrs. Bills puts all the things I ordered into the camper."

"Camper? What camper?" Cassa halted in the doorway.

Dan kissed her nose. "Didn't I tell you? I borrowed a camper from Phil Donner, one of my racquetball partners. We're going to camp overnight near the lake." He kissed her again and marched out of the room.

"But . . . but I don't like to camp," Cassa called after him.

Just then the phone rang. As she picked up in the bedroom, she heard Dan speak into the downstairs extension.

"Mr. Welles, this is Vince Laraby from Apex Alarm System. There was an attempted break-in at your place last evening. One of our dogs was hurt, but it doesn't look as though you've lost any merchandise. A Mr. Parnisian checked your stock and—"

"Fine," Dan cut in. "Dendor would know if anything was missing. I'll come right over. How's your dog?"

"Billy, the Doberman is fine, but Woolly, that fool Bouvier, got knocked in the head by one of the intruders. I don't think the dog was aggressive enough. I'll have to put him down."

"No!" Cassa shouted into the phone. "You can't. Dan, don't let him. We'll take the dog."

"Cassa, honey . . ."

"Ah, Mr. Welles, the dog is pretty even-tempered," Laraby said hesitantly.

"Now look, I'm not going to let my wife have a guard dog."

"Dan," Cassa wailed, "I want to at least see the dog. I'm coming down to the store with you."

On the way to the store Cassa overrode every objection Dan made.

"All right," he said finally. "We'll take a look at him, but if he's a tough customer, forget it."

"He'll be perfect, I just know it." Cassa leaned over and kissed her husband's cheek.

He frowned, shaking his head at her.

When they reached the store, a police car and an Apex Alarm van were parked there.

As Dan stopped to talk to Laraby and the policeman Cassa went into the store, where she found Dendor kneeling on the bare floor between rolls of carpeting. She looked over his shoulder. "Is this the dog, Dendor?"

He rose and moved away so she could see the animal that lay there motionless, his head on his paws.

"I haven't gotten too close, Cassa," said Dendor, "but he seems a gentleman to me." The old man's warm eyes returned to the dog.

Cassa craned her neck to get a better view. The big dog was brown with white spots and a wide, intelligent forehead. She clucked at him until he cocked his head to study her.

For several minutes the creature lay still, his face like a solemn bear's, his eyes alert. His hind quarters wriggled ever so slightly.

"He's wagging his tail!" Cassa exclaimed.

"Now, Cassa," Dendor cautioned, his gray eyebrows drawing together in concern.

For the first time Cassa noticed the gash over the dog's eyes. "Look at his head! He's bleeding. Nice baby. Shall I help you?" she crooned, moving past the protesting Dendor and kneeling beside the quiet dog.

The animal didn't stir, but his eyes followed her every movement. When she reached out a hand, he merely sniffed once.

"See, he wants me to help him." Cassa scrambled to her feet and rushed to the small bathroom, where she soaked a wash cloth in a solution of baking soda and warm water, then hurried back to the dog.

"Now, Cassa." Dendor lifted a cautioning hand.

"Dendor, please get the antibiotic ointment from the medicine chest. I forgot it."

The little Armenian shrugged and nodded. "But please be careful. I will be right back."

Cassa turned to the dog, murmuring endearments as she inched closer. At last she reached out a tentative hand and touched the wounded animal. His long tongue licked her, and she sighed with relief. "And they want to destroy you!" she said softly. "Well, I'm not going to let them," she promised, seating herself cross-legged in front of him and gently washing the gash on his head. When the dog remained quiet she moved even closer to study the wound more thoroughly. It didn't look very deep, she was happy to note.

She heard Dan's footsteps approaching from the back of the room, but she kept on working.

"If you give me a chance to look at the dog," he was saying to Laraby, "I'll decide if we can keep him. I won't allow my wife—" He gave a muffled curse, and Cassa knew he'd seen her. "Cassa, what the hell! Come here," he ordered, and lifted her right off the floor.

"Don't, Dan," she cried. "I'm all right. He's a gentle dog."

Dan held her struggling form close to him, his lips clamped shut as he imagined her being mangled by the dog's sharp teeth. His hands tightened on her. "No! I won't chance your getting hurt."

Cassa relaxed against him, as a feeling of safety, of homecoming, blossomed within her. "Then you look at him, silly. He's just a darling dog."

Dan set her behind him and knelt in front of the animal. He stoked the muzzle cautiously and checked him over, back to front. When Dan moved his hand near the animal's head, the dog gave a low growl.

"Dan, that's where he was hurt. Watch." Cassa crouched down beside her husband, and before he could stop her, she'd picked up the cloth and begun cleaning the wound. Although the animal whined once or twice, he made no threatening gestures.

"He's a good dog, I think," Dendor ventured after a moment.

"I agree." Dan nodded and rose. He turned to the burly man at his side. "Well, Mr. Laraby, what are you asking for him?"

"A good home." The man grinned. "I intended to put him down, so he's yours if you want him."

Cassa jumped to her feet and threw her arms around the man, kissing his cheek. "Thank you, thank you! I'll take good care of him." She smiled at Dendor, then turned to her husband. Her eyes widened in surprise at his obvious anger. His jaw was clenched tightly, and his neck was red.

Dan fought to restrain the jealous fury building inside him. Lord, he was paranoid about her. It tore him apart to see her give another man even a friendly kiss. He wanted to sock Laraby in the face!

When the Apex Alarms man left, Dendor watched as Cassa coaxed the dog to his feet. "My friend's son is a veterinarian—Larry Alisian. I can give him a call and ask him to take a look at the dog," Dendor offered.

Cassa said, "Thanks," and the old man went to make the call.

Dan returned from seeing Laraby to the door and shook his head. "You win, darling. We'll keep him. But I insist on monitoring his behavior very closely until I'm sure he's completely trustworthy."

She smiled and nodded.

"Where's Dendor?" Dan squatted down next to Cassa, kissing her cheek, then patting the animal.

"He went to call a vet named Larry Alisian to see if he can look at the dog right away. I hope he can." She rose with Dan, who was looking angry again.

"I thought we were leaving today for Darien Lake," he said.

"We are. Can't we get the dog checked first? Then we could take him with us."

Dan shrugged.

"You've been upset with me ever since Mr. Laraby said we could have the dog," Cassa ventured.

Dan's head whipped around. "There was no need for you to kiss Laraby. A simple thank you would have sufficed."

She covered her mouth to smother a giggle as he continued to glare at her. "Then you won't mind if we take the dog with us?" she asked sweetly.

"No," he barked. "We'll just have to find a trailer park that allows pets."

Cassa put her arms around his neck. "I'd rather you found a remote spot for the trailer, a place where we can be alone." She kissed his chin. "You're awfully silly sometimes." She kissed him again. "Dan, kissing Mr. Laraby might have been a bit impulsive of me, but I was just so glad the dog didn't have to be killed."

Dan's arms closed around her waist. He loved the feel of her against his body. He rubbed his chin on her hair. "I know. But I hate it when you kiss anyone but me." He gave her a wry smile. "We still don't know if he's a good animal or a cur."

"He's good, I just know it." Feeling jubilant, Cassa kissed her husband full on the mouth.

"Children, children." Dendor chuckled behind them. "You may take the dog to Larry Alisian now."

Neither Cassa nor Dan was sure the dog would come with them, but when they whistled and made beckoning gestures, he rose on shaky legs and followed them out to the car. The big Bouvier filled the entire back of the sports car, his big head hanging between them into the front seat.

"This should be loads of fun," Dan grumbled good-naturedly. "All the way to Darien Lake with King Kong between us." He raced the car down East Avenue to Chestnut

Street and from there to the expressway that would take them to Larry Alisian's veterinary hospital in the suburbs south of the city.

Larry pronounced the dog in good shape except for a slight concussion that required three stitches. There were also several contusions on his back where he'd apparently been struck with a blunt object.

"He may not be much of a fighter, but his friend the Doberman took care of the two men who broke in," Dan explained. "They were picked up by the police almost immediately when they sought treatment in the hospital."

Dan and Cassa returned to the car a few minutes later, and headed back toward home.

"I hope you realize that I'll have to run this fellow on the track over at the school to make sure he gets enough exercise," Dan said, giving Cassa a mischievous glance. "And you'll have to follow behind with a plastic bag to clean up after him. Cornhill expects its residents to be good neighbors." He laughed when she wrinkled her nose in distaste.

"I'll do my bit, but I won't like it," she promised, turning to their new pet. "How do you think you'll like living in a landmark neighborhood, Nappy?"

"Nappy?" Dan quizzed as he pulled into the driveway.

"Short for Napoleon. Even though Mr. Laraby said the breed is Belgian, a Bouvier des Flandres sounds elegant enough to deserve the name of a French emperor—voilà, Napoleon." Cassa grinned at her husband as he reached for the rope tied around the dog's neck.

Dan's heart lightened at the joy shining in his wife's eyes. She could keep this creature even if he turned out to be another Hound of the Baskervilles, he decided. He'd do anything to make her happy.

"Dan, let go of the rope and see if he'll follow me."

"Good grief," Dan grumbled, both amused and horrified as he imagined himself chasing the beast up and down the streets of Cornhill. But when he dropped the rope, Nappy remained where he was, his eyes darting questioningly from Dan to Cassa.

Cassa moved a few steps toward the house, and Nappy followed. "Isn't he brilliant?" she whispered to Dan.

"A regular Rhodes scholar," he agreed, sliding an arm around her shoulders.

Nappy lifted his lips and gave a low snarl.

Dan's head whipped around, his narrowed eyes fixed on the animal. "So, you think she's your girl, do you? Let me set you straight on that one, mister." Dan hugged Cassa close to him. "She's mine, and she always will be."

Nappy cocked his head thoughtfully. Then, apparently concluding that his mistress was in no danger, he yawned.

"I think you won that argument with him," Cassa said, laughing.

"There's no way I'd lose that argument with anyone, Mrs. Welles." Dan kissed her, his mouth moving sensuously against hers. "Come on, lady, we have to finish packing that trailer."

Cassa called to Nappy, who came at once. He followed her into the house, paused in the foyer, and then began a snuffling study of the premises. Finally he looked up at Cassa and uttered a low, mournful howl.

"Oh, poor baby. So sad." Cassa patted the dog consolingly.

"Sad? I think it's something more basic than that. C'mon boy, I'll introduce you to our back yard. You, wife, go over that checklist I left on the dresser."

With patient cooperation, sweat-producing labor, and some minor frustration, they managed to pack the two-bed camper with the collapsible roof. Then, putting the dog into the back seat, they climbed into the car and were on their way.

"Dan"—Cassa shot straight up in her seat, looking over her shoulder at the trailer behind them—"are you sure this car can pull that big thing?"

"Don't worry. I checked into it and had new shocks put on the car. We should be fine."

She sat back with a sign and closed her eyes.

"Tired, love?" He threw her a quick glance as they approached the expressway. Damn fool that I am! he thought. I shouldn't have let her do any of the packing. And I kept pushing her. His hands tightened on the steering wheel as he castigated himself.

"No, I may be a little sleepy, but I'm not tired," she

said. "It just seems so strange. Well, what I mean is..." She hesitated. "It's been so long since we went away—" She bit her lower lip.

"Together, you were going to say. I agree. It's about time we did something crazy and foolish, just the two of us—just us and *l'empereur* in the back seat, that is." Dan glanced in the rearview mirror and chuckled. "Damn. He sits taller than a man."

They traveled at a comfortable speed, stopping once to walk Nappy. Later they turned off at a sign that said: LOGAN'S WINERY ONE MILE and bought a jug of white wine.

Too soon for Cassa, the trip was over and they were searching for a campground that would accept dogs and wasn't too crowded. They found several that allowed pets, but the campers were all cheek by jowl with one another, and neither Dan nor Cassa wanted to stay.

Further down a country road not far from the amusement park they spotted a farm. Dan pulled into the driveway to ask the farmer, "Is there a less crowded place to camp in the area than the places near the lake?"

"Nope." Chewing on a bit of straw, the farmer leaned down and peered through the car window at Nappy, Cassa, and Dan. "Tell you what, though. When the missus was alive, she wanted me to start one of them campgrounds, crazy things that they are." He turned to spit a bit of straw out of his mouth. "I did it, but I didn't like it. When she died, I closed the place to campers. Still have electricity out there by the pond...even got a waterfall. You want to pay me ten bucks a night to stay there, you can, but don't tell your friends. They won't be welcome." The man took a deep breath, as though all that talking had tired him out.

"Could we look at it?" Dan asked, silencing Cassa's, "Oh, we'll take it," with a light squeeze of his hand on her thigh.

"Sure. Name's Calvin, Calvin Berry."

"Mine's Dan Welles, and this is my wife Cassa. The dog is called Nappy."

"Strange-looking critter, ain't he?" Farmer Berry blinked at Nappy, who stared alertly back. "I got me a dog. Was the wife's. A real killer she is too." He gestured with his piece of straw. "There's Sissy now."

Cassa's mouth dropped open as a fat chihuahua ambled down the driveway, wheezing and yipping.

"Fierce little beast, ain't she?" Farmer Berry stepped back from the car, chortling, and waved them toward a dirt road leading around one of the barns. "Go right to the end. Pond's there. Power's hooked up on one of the trees."

Dan nodded and drove forward slowly, the car dipping and swaying only slightly in the surprisingly smooth tractor track. "Umm. It looks as though Farmer Berry had this track graded," he said. "My car will be forever grateful."

"What did he mean, the power's in the tree?" Cassa asked, wincing as the trailer creaked.

Dan smiled at her, one hand leaving the gear shift for a moment to caress her knee. "There must be a power box affixed to one of the trees. Don't worry, love, we'll be fine."

Cassa admired the hilly pasture land, dotted here and there with apple and maple trees. "It's so free, so peaceful."

Dan clenched his teeth. She must be thinking of Suwanon. My sweet love, he vowed silently, no one is going to hurt you or intimidate you, or—his chest grew painfully tight—or take you against your will.

Cassa heard him groan and turned to him with concern, but when he pointed at the scene ahead, she was distracted. "The pond!" she exclaimed. "Look, there's the waterfall." About thirty feet high, the narrow stream of crystal-clear water spilled with a muted roar off the edge of the cliff and into the pond. As they watched, four geese rose into the air with honking protests and a whirr of wings.

Dan stopped the car at a flat area near a weeping willow, which curved out over the water. "I think this will do just fine, angel," he said, pulling the hand brake and stepping out. He came around to open her door and whistle to the dog. Holding Nappy's leash in one hand, he put the other arm around Cassa. "Welcome to paradise, Eve," he murmured into her hair, making her shiver. "I may decide to keep you here forever."

"You'll get no quarrel from me." She lifted her mouth and pressed it into his neck.

"Darling!" Dan gasped.

Nappy howled, making them jump apart.

"Fool." Dan scowled down at the dog.

"Time for another walk, I think." Cassa chuckled, her voice echoing in the verdant stillness. "I'll do it if you want to park the trailer someplace special."

Dan nodded, and looked about him. "How about there?" He pointed to a raised stretch of land not far from the waterfall but protected by the curve of rocky land that rose as a bed for the cataract. A large weeping willow provided an umbrella of shade.

Cassa nodded and turned at a tug of the leash to walk the anxious Bouvier. As she meandered along one side of the large pond, she was surprised and delighted to see how clean the water was. It was a good depth for swimming—if the water wasn't too cold. The last few days had been unusually warm, but it still might be too early in the season to plunge right in.

Cassa retraced her steps and joined her husband, who was raising the canvas top of the trailer. She paused to watch the strong play of muscles in his arms as he snapped the supports into place. Her heart pounded erratically at the thought of those same muscular arms closing around her body. Sweating and red-faced, Dan stepped back to admire his handiwork.

"Dan," Cassa called, and he turned inquiringly toward her. "The water doesn't seem to be too shallow," she said, tying the dog to the trailer door. "We seem to have our own swimming hole."

"Great. I think I'll use it now." He whipped off his shirt and tossed it to the ground, then began unfastening his jeans.

"Wait until I find your trunks," Cassa said, laughing at his impatience.

"No suits—for either of us, my sweet," Dan said with a leer, catching her by the arm when she would have moved away from him. With his free hand he unbuttoned her blouse and pulled it out of her slacks. When it fell open, he said softly, "No bra! Darling, how farsighted of you."

"Thank you," Cassa replied breathlessly. "Dan, we can't go skinny dipping here . . . can we?"

"Of course we can," he answered, distracted by her breasts. "They're so beautiful, so perfect. They've always been just like this—high with the nipples tilted up." His voice grew husky as his hands pulled her slacks down to her ankles and over her feet.

Except for her briefs, she stood there naked, gazing passionately up at him, thrilled by the smoldering look in his eyes.

"Maybe I should let you remove those, or we'll never go swimming," he muttered. When she began to edge the panties down her body, he stayed her hand. "No, no. Now that I have you back with me, I'm not going to deny myself any of the joys of your body." All at once his expression grew fierce. "I'll never let anyone near you again." He pulled her into his arms, mumbling endearments into her hair. "I could kill them, kill them all."

Cassa tried to lean back from him so she could see his face. "Dan, what—"

"No, don't pull away from me. I want to hold you." His grip tightened even more.

For long moments they stayed locked together. Then Dan moved back a fraction of an inch and dropped to one knee. He edged the briefs down her legs, leaning forward to kiss her inner thighs, making her whole body throb with desire. He lifted the panties over her feet and stood up. "You're very beautiful, Mrs. Welles."

"You look good to me, too," Cassa whispered.

"Good." He swept her up in his arms and carried her to the edge of the pond. He stood there for a moment, studying the bottom and shoreline, then waded into the clear green water. He drew in a sharp breath. "It's not freezing, but it isn't exactly tepid either." When he was waist-deep, he lowered her gently.

"It *is* freezing," Cassa cried, clutching his shoulders. "Ohhh, nice." She let her feet touch the silty bottom and gasped again. Then she ducked her face into the water and began to swim, feeling Dan at her side shortening his long, expert strokes to match hers.

Giddy with joy at being alone with Dan in this Garden of Eden, she turned and laughed at him through the water, grasping his head and dunking him.

His body went down easily, but he took her with him.

Then, floating closer, he pressed his mouth to hers. They rose to the surface, locked in a tight embrace.

Dan shifted onto his back, pulling Cassa on top of him, cushioning her. "Ummm, I like this, wife. Let me assure you that this cold shower is not having the usual effect."

"I noticed." She chuckled, blinking as the water waved gently around them, refracting the sunlight into a rainbow of colors.

For almost an hour they cavorted in the water like children. When Dan felt Cassa shiver, he swept her up in his arms once more and carried her across the grass verge to the trailer. Balancing her with one arm, he opened the door with the other.

"Dan, don't take me in there. It's all clean, and I'll drip," Cassa protested.

"Don't worry. I'll wipe up the puddles. It's too cool outside." He towelled her dry in the cozy kitchen area.

"How did you get a camper tall enough for you, Dan?"

"I borrowed it from a tall man."

Cassa grinned at him for no reason. "I like it here."

"I like it here too . . . with you," he said, rubbing her body with slow strokes.

"Me too! Being with you, I mean." She closed her eyes and leaned against his chest, trying to stifle a yawn.

"You're tired sweetheart. Shall we take a nap?"

"Aren't we going to the amusement park?" She yawned again.

"Later."

He urged her toward the double bed, pulled back the covers, and helped her slide between the sheets. His body curled around hers. "Um, lovely," Cassa murmured, her eyes closing. Immediately she fell into a deep and dreamless sleep.

Sometime later she awoke disoriented, but the heavy weight of Dan's body at her side immediately reassured her. Even as she shifted, his arm tightened around her middle.

"I was hoping you would wake up soon, before I had to take that dog for another walk around the pond." Dan propped himself up on one elbow and studied her face. "He seems content to stay with us, but I'm glad I brought that ground ring and chain so we can tie him in the shade." Dan nibbled her ear as his hand traced slow circles on her stomach.

"How smart of you," Cassa commented languidly.

"I thought so." His hands began a leisurely journey over her body, and she shivered with delight. His mouth followed his hands. "This is my favorite hobby," he crooned.

"I should think so." Cassa's laughter died in her throat as Dan increased the pace of his loving exploration.

Turning to pull her on top of him, he slid her velvet body up and down the length of his. "You are a perfect massage, my darling wife. I want you to cover me and hold me all the days of my life." His restless hands kneaded her rounded bottom.

Cassa grasped his face between her hands. "Are we going to talk? I'd much rather make love."

"I like to talk to you when I make—" Dan's words ended abruptly as Cassa slipped off his chest to lie beside him. He gave a soft moan as her hands began their own exploration down his lower body to caress, pull, and tug in sensual demand. "Oh, Dan . . ."

"No talking," he growled, his voice hoarse.

"That's what I said." She inhaled the damp maleness of his body as he writhed against her, the familiar scent making her own flesh come alive and acting as an erotic stimulus that both teased and tempted her.

Cassa felt a growing urge to both caress and possess him. She wanted to be all kinds of woman to him—to titillate, love, and soothe the man who was the center of her life.

She pushed a few inches back from him, wanting to see his magnificent, muscular body which had the strength of a weightlifter and the grace of a dancer. She wanted to play with the curling black hair that narrowed downward to his obviously aroused manhood. Her pulse was pounding out of control. "Do all married people love each other more every day?" she asked, voicing her thoughts without thinking.

"I thought you said no more talking."

"I changed my mind." Cassa chuckled, fingering the hard brown nipples on his chest, then leaning over to kiss them. "For so long I wanted to talk to you, to love you. Sometimes our life together seemed like a fantasy that I had stepped out of and was doomed to spend the rest of my life trying to get back into." Cassa's lips nibbled at the stubble of hair on his chin, and she saw his nostrils flare as her hand moved slowly down his body.

"I will never let any man touch or hurt you like that again," Dan promised, a sense of grief overwhelming him at the thought of all she had endured. He held her closer, his mouth descending to hers.

She raised her fingers on his lips, silencing him for a moment. "What do you mean?" Her breath caught as his hands pried gently between her thighs. But he ignored her question and she had no strength to pursue the issue as Dan slowly entered her. She was lost in a multicolored explosion of feeling as he filled her completely. She in turn enveloped him, caressed him, closed tight around him. The pulsating cadence took them away to another plane of existence.

"It's always perfect with you, my darling wife," Dan groaned as he drove into her for the ultimate completion.

Cassa tried to answer him, but no words came. She and Dan were united body and soul, as they climbed to the crest of love.

In the throbbing aftermath, she clung to him, wondering what it was she'd meant to ask him before passion swept them away. What was it she needed to know? In a sweet haze, she put the question aside and cuddled close to her husband.

"Are you going to sleep again, or are you going to let me get up and make us some dinner?" Dan purred in her ear.

"I was going to make love to you again," she dared to reply, finding a rich freedom, a wonderful release, in her lack of inhibition.

"In that case, forget the cooking," Dan muttered.

"We could cook together," she mused, stretching luxuriously.

He reached for her. "I thought we were going to forget about—"

Outside Nappy howled mournfully.

"That damned dog," Dan complained as Cassa chuckled

and rolled over him and out of bed. He reached for her as she stood up and stretched again. "Come back here. I'd rather have you than food, my love."

"That's nice." Cassa grinned, swaying toward him just as Nappy howled again. "Ooops, he must be hungry."

"I'll drown him in the pond," Dan grumbled, rising to his feet and flexing his arms.

Cassa's eyes were drawn like a magnet to his well-muscled torso. "You look so slender when you have your clothes on, Dan. No one would know what a hunk you are." Her eyebrows rose in astonishment as she saw a deep blush steal over his features. Why, he's embarrassed, she realized, though she knew, too, that he'd enjoyed the compliment. Impulsively she moved closer to him and pressed her mouth to his. Only their lips touched in the feather-light caress. "Time to fix our meal," she whispered.

Giving her one more hot glance he pulled on some clothes and went out to feed Nappy. Moments later Cassa heard him talking to the dog and whistling a cheerful tune as he ambled along the edge of the pond. She watched him through the window for a while, then turned her attention to more mundane concerns. She washed lettuce in the small sink, then sliced tomatoes, onions, and peppers for a salad.

When Dan returned, they worked together, bumping into each other now and then, delighting in the contact. Several times their eyes locked in happy contentment. Their meal would be simple but tasty. To go along with the salad, Dan wrapped chunks of haddock and scallops in aluminum foil with lemon, butter and black pepper. After setting the sealed packets aside next to a bottle of chilling wine, he helped Cassa scrape a bunch of carrots, some of which they ate. The rest they put into another foil packet with potatoes and onions. For dessert, they'd have grapes, Brie, and coffee.

They admired their work, then took the dog for another short walk while the vegetables cooked on the small outdoor brazier.

"Let's go back and put the fish on, then we can watch the sunset," Dan suggested.

Cassa nodded and yawned before she could stop herself. A second yawn followed. Dan slipped an arm around her waist, a crease of worry on his forehead as he studied her. "Still tired?" he asked casually, masking his concern. Had he worn her out? He shouldn't have been so demanding. He loved her, and it hurt him to think of the pain she had suffered.

Cassa shrugged. "Not tired, just lazy I think."

Halfway around the pond, Dan decided to release the dog from his lead. Nappy stayed near them, sniffing the ground. When Cassa gave Dan an "I-told-you-so" grin, he squeezed her hand and said, "It's a good sign, but remember he doesn't have his full strength back yet. He might wander farther when he feels better."

She shook her head. "No, he'll be good."

They returned to the camper. Dan served the food, placing it on the card table they'd set up under the porch canopy. Cassa arranged a few greens and wildflowers in a glass for an informal centerpiece, and brought out the salad and chilled wine.

Dinner was festive and fun. Cassa felt so close to Dan. The fetters of fear had fallen away.

"To you, darling, and to our life," Dan toasted her, clinking his glass against hers.

After they had cleaned up and put away the few dishes, they locked Nappy in the camper, telling him to lie down and rest.

The drive to the amusement park at Darien Lake was short. The park was still crowded with people, many of them families with children.

Cassa caught her breath at the sight of the huge Ferris wheel, but when she saw the roller coaster, she clapped her hands happily. "Look," she cried, grinning. "It's called The Viper!"

"You're acting like a little girl, wife of mine, not the twenty-seven-year-old co-proprietor of a thriving rug business," Dan said, delighted by her show of enthusiasm.

"I haven't been to an amusement park in years. I loved them when I was a child, but . . ." Cassa's voice faded as she stared, open-mouthed at the shrieking Viper passengers. All at once she felt a wave of nausea.

Dan leaned over her. "Let's walk around for a few minutes before we try anything, shall we?"

She nodded, her eyes on the long line of people waiting their turn at the roller coaster, and a few minutes later they found themselves in front of the ferris wheel.

"I think I'd like to try that," Cassa decided bravely.

"The Ferris wheel it is then," Dan said, buying two tickets.

The line wasn't nearly as long as the one for The Viper, but it was long enough for Cassa to observe the sea of faces around her. People were laughing, shouting, hollering, eating, drinking, and running. The jumbled sights and sounds made her head swim, which surprised her. Although she hated being penned in and alone, she had always been interested in people and had never minded crowds.

"It's our turn, Cass," Dan said, bringing her chin up with one finger so that he could look at her face. "Are you sure you want to do this? You look a little pale."

"Yes, I'm sure."

"Hey, mister, yer holdin' up the line," yelled a stocky man standing next to the ferris wheel. He was wearing a red T-shirt that said in big red letters: MY OLD LADY'S NO LADY. "Let's get movin' here or get outta the way." He shifted his half-smoked cigar from one corner of his mouth to the other.

"We're coming," Cassa answered, moving forward and allowing the muttering man to help her onto the seat.

As the man locked the bar across their laps, Cassa felt Dan's arm go around her, and the queasiness in her stomach subsided.

The Ferris wheel began its slow ascent as the man loaded and unloaded the seats. When they were more than halfway to the top, the wheel picked up speed and they traveled in continuous motion.

Cassa gasped fearfully as they crested the top and fell swiftly downward, but by the third time around she was crowing with delight. "Dan, isn't it wonderful?"

"You're wonderful, Cassa." He kissed her ear and, when the gondola swayed, laid his other hand across her middle.

"Lord, I'll lose my lunch, Lorraine!" the woman across from them announced with a pleased smile.

Cassa buried her face in Dan's neck. The mere suggestion had brought back her nausea. What was wrong with her?

She'd never been motion sick in her whole life! She clutched Dan's hand nervously.

"You'll be fine, love," Dan averred, his certainty comforting her.

"Yes." She swallowed. "Thank you, Dan."

"You're welcome, love." He kissed her on the mouth.

"Can't you save it till we're on the ground," the fat woman across from them muttered.

"Some people . . .!" Her friend Lorraine sniffed, then screamed as the ferris wheel whipped downward again.

When the ride was over, Dan kept his arm around Cassa as they descended the ramp. The two women who had been released after them followed behind.

"Hey, he's pretty cute," the fat one exclaimed.

"Yeah, he's a real sweet cheeks, ain't he." Lorraine snickered.

Laughter rose in Cassa as she looked up at Dan. He lifted his eyebrows and grinned. "Sweet cheeks, huh?" she teased. "Why, you old devil, charming those ladies." Cassa laughed out loud.

"They all love me. It's a burden I've had to learn to bear." Dan sighed mightily.

"You fool." Cassa punched his arm.

They didn't stay in the park long. The last light of day had just faded as they passed through the gates and headed back to camp.

"I'm glad we didn't stay in one of the trailer parks." Cassa shuddered at the noise and confusion of the crowded vehicles they passed.

"So am I."

When they reached their trailer, Nappy began barking from inside.

"Is he greeting us or warning us off?" Dan asked dryly.

"Don't be silly. He's happy to have us back." Cassa rubbed her forehead. "I feel grimy. Do you think we could take a bath in that oversize tub out there?" She pointed to the pond.

"That we can." Dan grinned at her as they approached the camper. When he opened the door, he was knocked backward as an exuberant Nappy leaped forward to welcome him home, licking Dan's face and wagging his tail in delight.

"All right, take it easy, chum." Dan laughed as he caught the big head in his hands.

"See, he's glad to see us!" Cassa cried, trying to avoid the animal's friendly wet tongue. "Do you think he'd like to swim with us?"

Dan cocked his head at the canine as he unbuttoned Cassa's blouse. "Maybe. I'll put him on the long lead and see if he'll follow us into the water."

"I can undress myself," she informed her husband, though she leaned against him cooperatively as he eased the slacks from her body.

"I know that." He kissed her nose. "Don't try to deprive me of the joys of being a husband."

"Is that what this is?"

"That's what it is." Dan's gaze grew hot as she stood naked before him. "Would you like to return the favor?"

They cavorted in the water for over an hour and, much to their surprise, Nappy eagerly joined them. Although Dan grumbled about the dog interfering when he wanted to make love to his wife in the water, Cassa wasn't disturbed: she could hear the happiness in his voice.

That night when they made love it was as though the whole world had faded away, and they were alone. Cassa truly felt that she was home, that Dan was hers. She fell easily asleep, safe and snug in his arms.

CASSA AWOKE THE next morning to the sound of birds singing. She breathed in the sweet scent of the meadow's wildflowers and grasses. But as she moved her head, a sudden queasiness swept over her. Almost gagging, she pulled herself erect and clambered over Dan to reach the camper's small commode, where she retched painfully. She was hardly aware of the cool hand that stroked her forehead or the strong arm that held her firmly around her waist.

"Darling," Dan whispered. "Are you all right?"

She nodded, unable to speak, and felt him lift her up and carry her to the bed. He placed her gently on the unmade sheets and leaned over her, concern etched sharply on his frowning face. As she looked up at him, a shocking thought made her blink in wonder. "Dan, could I be pregnant?" Stunned by her own words, she lifted a trembling hand to his cheek. "Wouldn't it be wonderful?" she breathed.

Dan's face went pale. He jerked away from her and sat down heavily. "How can you be sure? You haven't seen a doctor." Lord, he couldn't stand it! She'd been raped and now she was going to have a baby! As he watched her smiling radiantly up at him, he felt as if he were sinking into hell.

"No, I haven't seen a doctor, but sometimes a woman knows these things instinctively," Cassa said thoughtfully. Suddenly she was quite sure that she was indeed pregnant. Small signs, almost imperceptible changes in her body that she'd easily dismissed took on new signifigance, and she felt her heart soar. But as she searched Dan's face, she was alarmed by his sudden change of mood. "What's wrong? Don't you want a baby?"

He drew in a deep breath and caught her up in his arms, burying his face in her hair. "If you want the baby, we'll have it, darling. I . . . I just want you to be sure you're strong enough. I don't want anything to happen to you."

"Nothing will happen to me, Dan." Cassa lifted her arms and clung to him.

"You weren't doing too well a few minutes ago, were you?" he growled into her neck. Dammit to hell, he thought. She doesn't need this now.

"That's par for the course in pregnancy," Cassa assured him.

He lifted his head, his face still pale, his eyes dull. "So, you're an expert now?" he tried to tease her.

"Of course. All expectant ladies are experts in having babies. Don't you know that." She laughed, not feeling one bit queasy now.

"I'm just discovering it." He sighed, gazing at her lovingly. "You're sure you're all right? You really want this baby?"

Her heart sank as she said, "I want it, Dan, but if you don't, I—"

"I want what you want," he broke in, hugging her close again. "I want the baby, too." He rose, pulling the covers up around her. "New mamas get to stay in bed while new daddies make the breakfast."

"But I feel fine, Dan. Why don't you walk Nappy, and I'll get started in the kitchen. I don't want to stay in bed on such a lovely morning."

Dan studied her carefully, then said, "Let's plug in the coffee and both walk Nappy. We'll be ravenous by the time we get back."

As Cassa rose to her feet, a momentary dizziness came over again. "No, I'm fine," she said when he put his arms around her. She laid a restraining hand on his chest. "Really I am." She spread her arms wide, and went to the tiny sink to brush her teeth. "I think I'll take a quick swim before our walk, Dan," she called to him while drying her face.

"Good idea." He pushed back the folding door and stood naked in front of her. "I'm ready." He grinned at her, hiding his deep concern for her health.

"You wild man," Cassa teased as she took off her robe and prepared to join her husband for a morning dip.

As they left the camper, their arms around each other, Nappy strained at his leash and whimpered forlornly.

"Get your own girl, fool," Dan offered as Cassa laughed and released the dog.

"He'll stay with us without his lead," she said.

"I hope so." Dan ran a skeptical eye over the big brown-and-white dog. "I don't feel like chasing after him for miles," he said—but his thoughts were on Cassa, not the dog.

Nappy took a running leap into the water, his chin up, his legs working powerfully to bring him into the middle of the pond. He seemed to be fully recovered from his head wound.

"See, look how good a swimmer he is," Cassa exclaimed as Dan led her to the edge of the pond.

"Let's get in the water before that cur decides he wants to play fetch," Dan said, sweeping her up in his arms and carrying her into the water. "And don't say I don't have to carry you. I intend to carry you everywhere until I'm sure you're in very good health," he declared, his mouth tight. He let her slide down his body. "Why don't you call Nola Jacobsen when we get back home," he suggested. Nola was a friend of his from college who'd gone on to become an obstetrician.

"That's a good idea. I'll do it tomorrow."

They stayed in the pond for twenty minutes or so, Nappy frolicking at their side. After they got out and dried themselves, they decided to walk the dog before returning to the trailer for breakfast.

Nappy emerged and shook himself violently, sending a spray of water cascading over Dan. "Damn you, dog," Dan complained. "Did you have to do that all over me?" Cassa laughed helplessly, her hand over her mouth, and Dan couldn't suppress a grin. "Oh, lady mine, I do love the sound of your laughter." He moved closer to her. "But if you don't cover up that sexy body of yours, this poor dog will never get walked."

"Dan, don't look at me like that." Cassa was half amused, half startled by the sudden intensity of his gaze. His eyes were like a torch burning into her.

"You're so very beautiful, and you'll make a wonderful mother." His mouth tightened for a second, but then he smiled and led her back to the camper, where they dressed.

After a slow leisurely breakfast, they decided to relax in the sun rather than return to the amusement park. They lazed beside the pond all day, talking about the new baby, which Cassa was convinced would be a girl.

"Would you rather have a boy, Dan?" she asked from the haven of his arms.

"I want what you want, angel," he mumbled into her hair, his insides twisting painfully.

The rest of the day was warm and wonderful. It would have been perfect if Cassa hadn't felt a growing uneasiness, a conviction that Dan didn't really want the baby. Yet each time she broached the subject, he assured her he wanted what she wanted. Still, not once did he initiate any conversation about the birth of their first child.

They decided to drive home in the early evening. Despite the number of belongings they had strewn around their camping area, it didn't take them long to pack up.

When they stopped to pay Calvin Berry ten dollars for the use of his meadow they were treated to the sight of the aging chihuahua, which tried to attack Nappy, wheezing and barking furiously.

"Yup. Happens ever' time," said Mr. Berry. "No matter how big the young dog is, the older dog is the boss." He nodded sagely, tapped his dead pipe against the sole of his shoe, and waved good-bye.

"He was a nice man," Cassa said as they drove away. "Maybe we could go back next year—the three of us." Cassa studied Dan's face for some sign of his feelings.

For a moment his mouth looked hard, but then his lips softened and he nodded. "If that's what you want, darling." Oh, my angel, he thought, as long as you're fine, I'll love your baby.

Cassa tried to smile, but her chest felt tight with anxiety. She couldn't ignore his restraint.

They arrived home in the early evening to find a note from Mrs. Bills saying she'd left them individual chicken pot pies ready to pop in the oven, and a fresh apple pie for dessert.

After dinner Cassa buried her apprehension as she nestled in the crook of Dan's arm. They were sitting in the living room, thimble-sized liqueur glasses in their hands, Nappy lying at their feet. Matt the Cat was preparing for a night on the town by washing his paws.

"Uncle Aram was a wise man to put down so many bottles of Napoleon brandy, wasn't he?" Cassa observed, kissing her husband's throat.

"Love, don't do that. It might not be safe to make love now that you're pregnant and . . ." He fell silent. It panicked him to think that he might somehow cause her some harm. She had suffered far too much already.

"What?" Cassa stared at him in amazement. "That's the craziest thing I've ever heard in my life."

Dan's jaw hardened. "Until you see Nola and she gives the okay, I'm not touching you."

"Dan, that's ridiculous," Cassa wailed, punching his arm. "You can't be serious!"

She threw herself against his chest, pummeling him with her fists. He laughed, threading one hand through her hair. "Maybe so, but I'm still going to wait until Nola tells me it's all right."

"Dan, that could be weeks. I'm just a little bit pregnant, and she might not be able to see me right away," Cassa tried to explain.

Dan shook his head stubbornly. "I'll call her office tomorrow and make an appointment. I want you on vitamins and a special diet right away."

"Dan . . ." Cassa let out an exasperated breath. She knew it was no use arguing with him.

* * *

At work the next morning Cassa was about to bring up the subject again, but she decided to wait until Dan was finished going through the small mountain of mail that had accumulated in their absence. But by the time he was free, she was busy with two customers.

"I'm Mrs. Allen, and this is my sister Mrs. Vogt. I want to look at some oriental rugs."

"They get moths, Kay." Mrs. Vogt sniffed. "Horace says so."

"I'm here to buy orientals, Elaine," her sister insisted. "If you don't like it, you can wait in the car." She turned to Cassa. "I told her not to come. She prefers wall-to-wall carpeting."

"It wears better," Mrs. Vogt said, glaring at Cassa. "Floors get dusty."

Cassa noted the militant look in Mrs. Vogt's eyes and chose not to argue with her. "It's all a matter of taste," she said, wishing Mrs. Allen had left her bellicose sister at home. Mrs. Allen interrupted her thoughts by pointing to a brilliant red Sarouk with a border of green, pink, cream, and black. It was one of Cassa's favorites.

"As you can see, this rug is tightly woven," Cassa commented. "Like many fine oriental carpets, it was woven by children. Sometimes their hands become almost arthritic from doing this work, but the knots are all perfect." Seeing the horrified look on her customer's face, Cassa hurried on to explain. "I know it sounds like child abuse, but I've heard that the people tend to have very close family ties. If the children are happy and well loved, their lives can't be so terrible. Middle Eastern youngsters have been weaving rugs for centuries."

"That is the ugliest thing I've ever seen," said Mrs. Vogt. "It should be hung in a carnival. I'm going to the car." And with one last snort of disgust, she marched out the front door.

Mrs. Allen sighed. "My sister can sometimes be a bit strong-minded," she told Cassa apologetically.

Bullheaded is what she is, Cassa thought. But she smiled at Mrs. Allen, and kept her thoughts to herself.

"Darling . . ." Dan suddenly appeared at her side. "I don't

like to disturb you, but I thought you should know I called Nola Jacobsen. You have an appointment for next week. I told her I'd be bringing you." He kissed her surprised mouth, smiled at Mrs. Allen, and excused himself.

Cassa's customer smiled back indulgently, then gave her full attention to three rugs: a Bokhara, an Isfahan, and a Chinese. But she kept returning to the ruby-red Sarouk. "It's so warm, so welcoming." She sighed. "It's more money than I planned on spending, but—" She bit her lip, then nodded. "I'll take it. Young lady, you're a good saleswoman. So patient."

Cassa was delighted with the sale of such a large carpet. But, as always when she sold one of the larger rugs, she experienced a sense of loss. The carpets were more than a combination of splendid colors, intricate knots, and beautiful designs. They were works of art, and she felt respectful and protective of them—almost as if they were children. Instinctively her right hand pressed flat against her abdomen. She was having a baby.

Entering the office, Cassa saw Dan bent over the ledgers and order books. Such a rush of love swept over her that she was glad he didn't turn around and look at her. She might have jumped into his lap and told him to take her home and make love to her.

In the days that followed, a frustrated Cassa tried all her wiles on Dan, but nothing would budge him from the stand he'd taken against having sex until she'd seen the doctor. Her irritation mounted, and by the day of her first examination, she was ready to throw him through a window.

They rode in silence to the medical building, where Nola's office was located. While Dan parked the car, Cassa entered the waiting room and took a chair, half smiling at the only other occupant, a very pregnant woman, who disappeared into the inner office just as the receptionist called Cassa to the desk.

"Mrs. Welles? Good. Would you fill out this form for us, please? The doctor will see you in just a moment."

"Thank you." Cassa resumed her seat just as Dan came in. He sat down next to her and glanced at the form.

"Dan, it's silly for you to wait here," Cassa protested. "I can call a cab."

"No problem. Dendor likes to handle the store on his own, and he does it better than either one of us." Dan motioned for her to continue writing.

"Mrs. Welles, Dr. Jacobsen will see you now. Ah, Mr. Welles, you can wait—"

"I'd like to speak to the doctor," Dan informed the nurse imperiously.

Cassa smiled weakly at the nurse and preceded Dan into the office, where the smiling doctor awaited them.

Nola Jacobsen was a tall, spare woman whose blond hair was sprinkled with gray. She had slightly freckled skin and bright green eyes. As she came around the desk, her hands outstretched in greeting, she shook her head. "I see you haven't changed, Dan Welles. Still riding roughshod over the opposition. If you've given my receptionist palpitations, I'll sue you." She kissed Cassa on the cheek. "So . . ." She indicated two chairs in front of her desk. "I was a bit surprised when you said you were coming in with Cassa, Dan. Is there some special problem I should know about?"

"Of course there's no problem," Cassa began. "I'm only a few weeks—"

"There could be problems," Dan interrupted. "My wife suffered a terrible ordeal during the nine months she was held incommunicado in Suwanon. I just want to make sure there are no . . . complications."

Nola's eyes narrowed as she studied him, but then she smiled and turned to Cassa, who sat red-faced and uncomfortable. "All right, I'll examine her, and then we'll talk." She gave Dan a sardonic grin. "You *will* let me examine her in private, won't you?"

He hesitated.

Cassa bit her lip. "Of course he will. We'll be right back, Dan."

She followed a nurse to an examining room and was lying under a white sheet staring up at the acoustical ceiling when the doctor returned. During the examination, Nola kept up a stream of casual conversation which helped Cassa relax.

Finally Cassa broached the subject that had been uppermost in her mind for the past week.

"Nola," she said, a blush suffusing her pale cheeks. "Dan won't make love to me unless you give him written permission." Despite her embarrassment, Cassa had to smile when Nola laughed out loud.

"You're fine, and it's all right to make love," Nola assured her.

Finally the doctor finished. Cassa sat up and swung her feet over the side of the table. "I don't know what's gotten into Dan." She bit her lip. "He keeps saying he wants what I want, but he's never actually said he wants the baby."

"Well, of course I haven't discussed that with him, Cassa. But I do know one thing: that man is madly in love with you."

Cassa nodded. "I know. I love him too." Her voice trailed off. She couldn't say anything more, not even to the doctor, about her feelings for Dan and the baby.

"Get dressed, Cassa. I'll talk to you both as soon as you've dressed." Nola left the room while Cassa got back into her clothes.

When she returned to the office, Dan rose and came forward to kiss her mouth. "Are you all right, darling?"

"I'm fine." She leaned closer and whispered, "And we can make love. Nola okayed it." She grinned up at him as his neck turned red. "I told her you were anxious," she teased.

"Cassa," Dan growled, clearly embarrassed.

Just then, Nola returned. "Cassa gets a clean bill from me," she announced. "She's anywhere from four to eight weeks pregnant."

"Is she okay? That's my only worry," Dan said sharply. Cassa had been back seven weeks. She must have been raped just before she'd been released.

Both Cassa and Nola looked at him quizzically.

"Cassa is in very good shape," Nola reiterated. She then proceeded to outline an exercise program and diet plan.

To Cassa's amazement, Dan not only took great interest in every word the doctor said, but also insisted on stopping at a pharmacy on the way back to work to get her vitamins.

"Maybe you shouldn't go back to work," he said, pulling out of the pharmacy parking lot.

"Dan, don't be silly. I'd go crazy if I didn't work." Cassa patted his arm.

"Well, just as long as you're all right." He gripped her hand tightly.

"I'm fine." Cassa was touched by his concern, but puzzled as well. "I'm looking forward to our night on the town. Don't forget that we're meeting Maddy and Gir for drinks at Denny's," she reminded him.

"Yes, I know. I asked Len to join us." Dan shrugged when she frowned. "Maddy and Len have gotten together a few times. I admit I don't like playing the role of matchmaker, but that's the least I can do for them. You can't imagine how many hours they spent listening to me rave about you when we first began dating. They didn't even laugh—well, only a little."

"They didn't!" Cassa felt covered in soft, warm velvet.

"Yes, they did. And don't forget how many times they invited us to dinner, and then left so we could be alone." Dan parked the car in Parson's Alley and came around to open her door.

"Well, I hope they'll both be on their best behavior at Denny's. I would hate to find myself in the middle of a fight." Cassa chuckled.

"Bar-room brawls are off-limits to pregnant ladies," Dan announced.

Business was good that afternoon, and Dan was still busy with a customer when Dendor waved good-bye at five o'clock.

By the time Dan was free, Cassa had completed the day's logging and straightened up the office.

Dan took time for a quick shave, and then they had to rush to meet Maddy, Gir, and Len at Denny's, a local bar, located on Main Street.

When Dan opened the doors, music, laughter, and conversation assailed them. They had to stop often on their way to the bar to greet acquaintances. By the time they reached the niche at the oaken bar that had always been their special spot, Maddy and the two men were already sipping their drinks.

Maddy scowled at Cassa and asked the bartender for another martini.

"Maddy," Len interjected softly, "you'll fall flat on your lovely bottom if you finish that." He took her arm and pulled her close to him.

"I need the courage," she said flatly.

Gir gulped the last of his rum and branch water and said, "Sorry, I've got to run. I have a racquetball match in twenty minutes. Of course I'll win."

"Bull," Cassa pronounced inelegantly.

Maddy gave him a loud "razzberry," and they all four turned to stare at her in surprise. "I've always wanted to do that," she explained, lifting her chin.

"Good Lord, she's smashed," Gir announced. He kissed her cheek, then Cassa's, waved at the two men, and left.

"Not smashed . . . am I, Cass?" A single tear trickled down Maddy's cheek.

"Smashed," Len confirmed.

"Why don't we take her to our house for dinner," Cassa offered. "She'll be fine as soon as she eats."

"Good. I'll drive her there and take her home later," Len announced, brooking no protests.

"Fine." Dan took Cassa's arm. "Let's leave now."

On the short walk back to the car, Dan chuckled and said, "If Maddy needed that drink for courage, she must be ready for a big confrontation with Len. She's not going to find it easy to enunciate her words, whatever she has to say."

"It's not funny," Cassa said, but she couldn't help smiling as they got into the car and drove along Exchange Street toward home. "Maddy never has been much of a drinker," she admitted.

They arrived home to find that Mrs. Bills had left them strawberry soup, homemade rolls, and a chicken casserole with carrots and dumplings.

"Umm." Len sniffed appreciatively as he entered the house without knocking, his hand on Maddy's arm. "Mrs. Bills is a jewel. I'm so damned sick of eating out, I could strangle a maître d' without a qualm."

Dinner was ready to eat in short order, and soon the four of them were sitting down to an endive-and-onion salad, cold beets in vinegar, the chicken casserole, and white wine.

When Maddy held out her wineglass, Len shook his head no. Again one tear slipped down her face.

"Len, I'll never be able to tell you what I have to tell you if I'm sober."

His face turned white. Cassa sucked in her breath. "Now what?" Dan muttered.

"Just say what you have to say, Mad," Len urged. "I won't get angry, I promise."

"But will you stay married to me?" She drew in a shuddering breath. "You asked me, but I didn't know if you still wanted me . . . and I've decided that I will trust you . . . because I know I can't live without you and be happy. But please don't feel—"

Len leaped to his feet, knocking his chair over backward.

"Easy on the furniture, friend," Dan smilingly cautioned him.

Len came around to Maddy's chair and lifted her into his arms. "I'll give you one hour to get cold sober. In the meantime, I'll book us a flight to St. Thomas. We're going on a second honeymoon, and we'll never be separated again, my love." And turning to Cassa, he barked, "Give her some coffee—quick!"

"Bossy," Maddy muttered, slackjawed as Len dumped her unceremoniously back in her seat and headed for the phone in the den.

She rolled her eyes toward Dan and Cassa. "You understand, don't you? I could never have proposed to him without dutch courage, could I?"

"Never," Dan agreed soothingly, pouring her a cup of coffee from the silver pot, then spooning some of the chicken casserole onto her plate.

"I'm certainly glad Len's parents aren't here to see their daughter-in-law drunk." Maddy stared moodily into her coffee cup.

"They always thought you were perfect, Maddy," Cassa assured her. "Are you sure this is what you want, Maddy?" she whispered.

"Yes, I am. I remember what you said about Dan, how he was the center of your life. Len is my center." She nodded firmly. "We'll work out the problems."

Dan came around to Cassa's chair and bent over to kiss her hair. "I like being the center of your life, angel."

Len raced back into the room, his eyes darting at once to his wife. "The arrangements are all made, Mad. Tomorrow we'll be on our way to the Caribbean."

"Dan and Cassa should come too," Maddy said nervously.

"We can't, Maddy. We've spent too much time away from the store lately," Dan began, sending Cassa a questioning glance. At her nod he added, "Besides, I don't want my pregnant wife to travel." He grinned as Len let out a loud whoop and Maddy began to cry in earnest.

"When?" Maddy asked, gulping.

"February fifth, I think." All at once Cassa felt teary-eyed too. "I want you both to be godparents."

"That's beautiful," Maddy wailed, sobbing into her napkin.

"Honey, it's wonderful," Len enthused, going over to kiss her cheek, then pumping Dan's hand.

Maddy's eyes locked on Len's. "I want a baby too."

Dan laughed out loud, and Cassa giggled. Len leaned tenderly over his wife to murmur, "I'll start working on it tonight, if you like."

"Thank you." Maddy sighed. "But could you let me go for now? I'd like to finish eating."

They all laughed again, and later Dan brought out a chilled bottle of champagne. Maddy settled for a goblet of white grape juice.

Maddy and Len left soon afterward, Len assuring Maddy that there was no need to pack many clothes since he would buy her anything she needed when they got to St. Thomas. Dan would tell Gir about their plans first thing in the morning.

After they left, Dan and Cassa cleared the table in a companionable silence. Every few minutes Dan would stop what he was doing and stare at Cassa. Each time she met his gaze, he smiled. But occasionally she caught a brief glimpse of pain on his face. He was doing a good job of hiding it, but she was sure that something was bothering him.

"Dan..." Cassa stepped in front of him. "Wouldn't it

be wonderful if Maddy did get pregnant right away? Then our child would have a playmate."

All of his attention seemed to be focused on picking up as many dessert plates as he could carry. "Sure. Ah . . . you want to wash the good china by hand, don't you?"

He headed from the dining room into the kitchen, and moments later Cassa heard him running water in the sink. Her eyes wandered over the beautiful room that she and Dan had decorated together, taking in the gilt-edged high ceiling, the antique crystal chandelier, the grass clother wallpaper in pale cream with fern fronds in a deeper cream, the wall-sized bay window with its solid oak bench almost buried under a profusion of blue velvet cushions. But she found no contentment in the room. The swagged peach, blue, and cream drapes didn't make her smile, as they usually did. And this time even the gorgeous oval Kerman on the floor failed to soothe her. Why wouldn't Dan discuss the baby with her? Why was he pretending to want it when it seemed obvious to her that he didn't?

Cassa shook her head and entered the kitchen, where her husband was standing in front of the sink, a bibbed denim apron protecting his shirt and trousers, his forearms buried in suds.

He turned to her and said, "Why don't you go on up to bed? I'll finish here." Was she a little pale? he wondered, worried.

Cassa shook her head. "No. I'll dry."

Reluctantly Dan said, "All right . . . if you're sure you're not tired." Maybe he should insist she stop working at the store.

"Have you started the dishwasher?"

"I was just going to."

The muted roar of the machine kept conversation to a minimum as they finished putting the Haviland china back in the ornate, rosewood breakfront that had belonged to Uncle Aram. Then they turned out the lights downstairs and headed toward the floating staircase.

Cassa paused on the first step and turned to Dan. He leaned toward her, and she felt warmed by his smile. "Please . . . tell me Dan, what's wrong? About the baby, I mean. I—"

He pulled her close, his face a bronze mask in the light cast by thc amber-and-brass sconces on the wall. "Nothing is the matter, darling. I promise you that. Perhaps I'm not used to the idea of becoming a parent yet, but I swear I'll be the best father any child ever had."

"Is that what it is? Are you nervous about becoming a father?" Cassa laughed, eagerly accepting his explanation.

"It's a big step in our life together." He nuzzled her neck. "Now, do you mind if we hurry a little? Nola did say we could make love, and I've been thinking about that all day, woman." No matter what it took, he vowed to himself, he would love this baby.

"Insatiable, that's what you are." Cassa sighed as Dan cradled her close to him. Slowly, their hips bumping, they walked up the last steps to the hall, then to their bedroom.

"Would you like to soak in the hot tub?" Dan asked as Cassa began unbuttoning his shirt.

"Yes, I would." She beamed at him, loving his hot, passionate expression. "Dan, when I was in Suwanon, I used to dream about the first time you made love to me. I would recall every minute, each detail." She leaned slightly away from him. "You were more nervous than I was."

He nodded ruefully. "I was. I was desperate to please you, but I knew that for most women the first time is uncomfortable. I wanted to be your first and only." His eyes glinted hard for a moment, and then he was smiling again.

"I enjoyed it—even the first time," she assured him earnestly.

"Hussy."

"Yes." Cassa laughed. "When we were first married, I used to try to think of ways to get you into bed."

"Lord, darling, all you had to do was look at me. All I had to do was think about you. And when you walked in front of me"—he made a helpless gesture—"I'd forget what I was saying to customers, whether they were on the phone or on the floor." He grinned as she stood before him clad only in her bra and panties. "We certainly didn't eat much when we had lunch at home, did we?"

"Not true," Cassa disagreed, following him into their bathroom and submerging herself in the churning hot tub. "Ahhh. This is heaven."

"At times you are a true hedonist, my love." Dan shifted and pulled her under him. "Ahhh. Now that's what I enjoy . . . your luscious bottom in my lap."

"You're not acting like the very conservative vendor of fine carpets who owns stores in Syracuse, Buffalo, and Rochester," Cassa teased. She gasped as his hands claimed her.

"With you I never feel the least bit conservative. Wild is more like it. And, if anything, I'm getting worse." He smiled sardonically, making her laugh. "Have you no pity, beautiful lady of my life?" But her laughter was a balm to his spirit.

"None. I like you this way," Cassa burbled, bubbling over with unrestrained happiness.

Rising like Poseidon from the sea, Dan lifted her free of the foaming water and stared down at her. "I'm going to make you happy every day you live, my own darling," he vowed solemnly.

"You do make me happy, Dan," she said, clasping her damp arms around his neck.

He let her slip down his body, and his hair-roughened body felt pleasantly abrasive on hers. "Do I, my treasure? Good, because you're my source of happiness. I learned that at great cost." His face contorted. Even as Cassa watched him, his color seemed to drain away.

"It's over, Dan. The bad time is over." Her voice was barely audible as she whispered into his ear.

"Yes." He dried her gently with a soft towel, his mouth following his hands to lick up any trace of moisture he had missed.

As he continued his fondling long after her very core had turned to warm honey, she grew fiercely impatient and gripped him with a strength born of passion. Her mouth moved over his chest in ardent exploration. "I love you very much," she announced with the clarity of a bell pealing out the words.

"I'm so glad of that, Cassa, you imp, you wanton witch."

Dan gasped as she continued to taste and caress him with all her skill and energy. At last he carefully urged her onto her back, holding her like a precious treasure in his hands.

"You're my delight, my joy. But you, you gorgeous creature, are also my torment; if I don't have you now, I'm going to explode."

He joined their bodies with a slow, heart-stopping thrust. Gradually the tempo of his powerful strokes quickened. Relentlessly the colorful spiral of tension grew and grew, taking them out of themselves once again. Their love pounded in a primitive cadence as they strained together toward the fulfillment that came at last in a glorious release.

Much later Cassa first became aware of Dan's heart thudding under her cheek. "You're terribly good at this," she told him lazily, kissing his shoulder.

"So are you, my darling wife. I love you, Cassa." He kissed her eyes closed, and leaned down to capture her mouth.

8

IN THE MONTHS that followed, Cassa became more aware of her body and of the new life growing within her. Though she still sensed Dan's ambivalence toward the baby, she couldn't fault his solicitous care. If anything, he was overly protective.

At the store he watched over her like a mother hen, not letting her lift anything or tire herself. Even when he visited the other stores in Syracuse and Buffalo, he telephoned frequently to make sure she was all right. And he wasn't above calling Nola Jacobsen if he felt anything was wrong. When Cassa protested, he overrode her objections. She tried turning to Dendor for help, but found that he was almost as bad as Dan. By October, her fifth month of pregnancy, she was straining under his restrictions. Len also came into the store or called almost daily to see how she was. Most days she met Maddy for lunch, since Dan had many business lunches and was often out of town.

"Honestly, Maddy, he's too much," Cassa grumbled good-naturedly over a healthful lunch of tuna salad, skim milk, and applesauce. "You certainly look sunshiny today. Not that you haven't looked that way the entire four months since your reconciliation with Len. And I think he looks even happier than you do." She scooped up the last bite of applesauce. "I hope I can keep from gaining too much weight. The food that's good for me is just so good!" She patted her generously rounded stomach.

Maddy leaned forward, her eyes bright. "Len and I are trying for a baby, Cass. I just know we'll have one soon. Actually, I'm three days late, and you know how regular I am." When Cassa laughed, Maddy glared at her. "Stop laughing." She propped her chin on her hand. "Lord, Cass, can you imagine a baby boy just like Lennie?" She sighed and took a long drink of iced tea.

Cassa laughed at her sister-in-law's dreamy expression, but she nodded in agreement. "It is exciting. Sometimes I could just shout out loud for happiness." But her smile faded. "I just wish the father . . ." She bit her lip.

"Now Cass." Maddy regarded her sternly. "You don't still think Dan doesn't want the baby, do you? Because if you do, you're crazy. Dan loves kids."

"Yes, he does." But for some reason, he doesn't want this one, she couldn't help thinking.

When they left the restaurant, Maddy insisted that Cassa come back with her to the store. "Gir is absolutely repelled by maternity clothes, as you know, but"—Maddy glanced mischievously at Cassa as they strolled toward the mall—"even though he won't admit it, he's thrilled that you're going to make him the baby's third godparent. He just returned from a fabric-buying trip to New York with a huge box full of maternity clothes . . . all in your size." Maddy and Cassa laughed.

"Did he really?" Cassa asked.

"Cross my heart." Maddy's eyes brimmed with amusement as they entered her busy boutique. The two saleswomen Maddy had hired to help out were busy with customers, and another woman was waiting impatiently for someone to write up her purchases.

"Go right back," Maddy whispered. "I'll take care of the customer."

Cassa walked into Gir's workroom at the back of the shop to find him bent over some swatches of material, mumbling to himself.

"If that's you, Madeleine Louise, you are five minutes late and there's another customer out there. I do not intend to wait on the plebeians." Scowling, he studied the fabrics in front of him.

"Grouch," Cassa muttered in his ear, making him jump.

"Damn you, Cassa, you startled me," Girardot said mildly, smiling and shaking his head. "You look like a kangaroo with a baby in your pouch. In fact, you will continue to look disgraceful until you start wearing some decent maternity clothes. I'm surprised the besotted Dan Welles hasn't already bought you a closetful." He ignored her glare and jerked his head toward a fitting room. "Try on the samples I brought."

"First I'd better call Dendor and tell him where I am so he doesn't worry."

Gir shrugged and pointed toward the wall phone.

Dendor answered on the first ring, and they exchanged quick greetings.

"...No, I won't be too long," Gir heard Cassa say. "What?... You did! How wonderful!" Cassa hung up the phone. "Gir, guess what? Dendor sold three large Bokhara carpets to the Faculty Club. Isn't that great?"

"Please, Cass, don't bore me with endless tales of that prosaic business." Gir gestured impatiently toward the fitting room, then whirled around on his high stool and got right back to work.

She was about to retort when she realized he was already lost in contemplation of his fabrics.

The minute she entered the fitting room Cassa let out a gasp of amazement. Maternity suits, dresses, and coats hung all around the mirrored room. "Gir," she called, "I can't take these. Dan would have a fit."

"Tell him to stuff it. He should have bought you some decent things weeks ago."

"He wanted to, but I preferred not to buy too much. I'd rather wait until after the baby is born." Cassa's temper was rising at Gir's criticism of Dan. "What's more, Dan's always buying me things."

"Stop shouting and try on the clothes."

"Someday someone's going to strangle you," she muttered, pulling a red silk jumper over her head. It settled in soft folds over her burgeoning frame.

For forty-five minutes she changed in and out of outfits, finding each one more delightful than the last.

She finally emerged from the dressing room, hot and rumpled but pleased with Gir's choices. She couldn't decide which ones to take.

"I can't make up my mind, Gir." She sighed. "You choose for me."

"Simple. They all belong to you," he answered without looking up from his worktable.

Cassa had been afraid of this. "I can't accept all these expensive clothes!"

"Then throw them away," Gir retorted, a drawing pencil in his mouth.

"Don't be ridiculous," Cassa retorted. She paused. "If Maddy gets pregnant, I could give them to her." She stopped when he whirled on his stool again to glare at her.

"If you're suggesting that any of these clothes would suit Madeleine Louise—if and when she becomes enceinte—then you are more a fool than even I supposed . . . and you damn well shouldn't be dealing in oriental carpets." Gir's tone was scathing.

"I have very good color sense," Cassa shot back, stung.

"Then you damn well should know that gem-bright colors of red, orange, and lemon yellow would not do at all with Maddy's dark blond coloring. They look good on brunettes—you, in particular, with your smoke-gray eyes." He studied her critically. "Though when you are more pleasant-natured, which is rare, of course, your eyes are actually blue-green."

"Idiot." Cassa was seething.

"Fool," Gir replied. "Take them; they're yours. One of

my wholesalers in New York was more than happy to let me have them for almost nothing when he saw the huge order I gave him. Besides, I told him that you'd be a walking advertisement for his work." Gir shrugged. "He was delighted. And don't you worry, my pet, if the lovely Madeleine becomes pregnant, I shall do the same for her."

Just then Maddy tottered toward them on her high heels, looking totally frazzled. "Women! Why must they be so difficult?"

"Because it's their nature," Gir answered, earning glares from both Cassa and Maddy. "By the way, Cassa, go back and change into the orange suit . . . and throw away that thing you're wearing. It offends me."

"What's wrong with this? I got it on sale. It was a great bargain." Cassa bristled.

"Where?" Gir scoffed. "At the Salvation Army? Maddy, rip the rag off her at once."

"Better not argue with Caesar," Maddy advised, leading her back into the dressing room.

"Maddy, he's given me too much. And he said he's going to do the same for you when you get pregnant." Cass grinned.

Maddy sighed. "Soon, I hope."

The two women hugged each other, and then Maddy helped Cassa get into the bright orange suit.

Maddy stepped back and shook her head. "You look gorgeous. Good enough to eat. Your hair's so shiny black and wavy, and your eyes look almost silver. It's a good thing you wore the beige shoes today. They go well—"

"Did you think I would tell her to wear something that didn't coordinate with her shoes?" Gir roared from the workroom.

"A pox on thee, Caesar," Cassa shouted, chuckling.

Maddy grimaced in her associate's direction, then turned back to Cassa. "You're beginning to show quite a bit, but your hips don't seem any wider."

Cassa patted her stomach. "I'm carrying it all here . . . and here." She slapped her backside.

"Your skin is so pearly and clear, and your eyes have a dreamy sparkle to them. You were always lovely, Cass, but now you're . . ." Maddy shrugged, gesturing for Cassa to precede her out of the dressing room.

"Ethereal is the word you're searching for, little Madeleine," Gir said. "And I hope you burned that awful sack she was wearing."

"I did not." Maddy gave him a sharp look, and then her eyes narrowed. "I told Cass to keep it—to garden in." She winked at a glowering Cassa.

Gir studied Cassa's outfit thoughtfully. "Not bad." Ignoring her fulminating look, he added, "Please close the door to the sale room when you and Maddy leave. The noise is awful today."

Cassa gave him a puzzled look and turned to Maddy. "You can hardly hear a pin drop in here," she whispered.

"I heard that, idiot child. Now get out of my domain and back to your rug merchant. Ugh, what a trade."

Cassa wheeled about to do battle with him about his disparaging remarks—not only about her darling Dan, but also about her chosen life's work. But Maddy caught her around the waist. "Ignore him. He enjoys baiting the people he loves—and of course he's managed to avoid having to listen to your thanks."

Cassa groaned. "I *didn't* thank him. Damn the man! He's outrageous." Then she got an idea. "Wait here for a moment, sister dear." She ran back to Gir and, before he could turn on his stool, gave him a smacking kiss on the cheek. "Thank you, my cutesy, sweetums friend," she said saccharinely.

"Aaagh, you simpering witch! How dare you!" Gir laughed and tried to tickle her, but Cassa broke free, chuckling.

Rejoining Maddy, she slapped her hands together in a gesture that said, "mission accomplished."

Laughing, Maddy led her toward the front of the store. "Since Dan will be out of town tonight, why not join us for dinner. We're having clams casino to start, then red snapper and new peas, and the Pear D'Anjou Chocolat for dessert," Maddy said, teasing Cassa, who was on a strict diet.

"Stop! My taste buds are in extremis. No wonder my brother looks so happy. He has his cook back."

"Oh, Cass." Maddy sighed. "It's so nice to be with him again. At first I'd wake up and think I was dreaming. Perhaps I'll get used to it when we've been married fifty years." She waved good-bye to Cassa and greeted a new customer without skipping a beat.

Cassa hurried back to Tijanian's flushed with delight at the thought of all her new clothes, her body feeling less cumbersome in the loose orange outfit. When she greeted Dan with an exuberant hug, he wrapped his strong arms around her, pressing her back against his chest. "I thought you'd gotten lost," he muttered, his lips on her neck. Suddenly he stiffened. "You're too warm. Have you been rushing?"

"Dan." Cassa turned awkwardly in his arms, her protruding tummy pushing them slightly apart. "I'm as healthy as a horse. I could run up the side of Whiteface Mountain if I chose." She lifted her arms to his neck.

"I don't want you exerting yourself." Dan's jaw hardened, and he felt a familiar curl of desire as he looked down at her. She looked even more gorgeous than usual today. "Honey, I don't remember that outfit, but it suits you to a tee."

"Thank you. Gir brought it back from New York."

"Gir bought this?" Dan's voice had hardened.

Cassa put an index finger on his lips. "Don't get excited, please. Gir brought back some sample dresses from one of the fashion houses he deals with. He purchased a great deal of fabric, so he was able to get a good deal on the clothes."

"Clothes? How many things are there? And how much do I owe him?"

"You owe him nothing. The clothes are a gift."

"No."

Even as he said the word, he knew he was being unreasonable. Jealous bastard! he castigated himself. But the knot of insecurity remained. Although Cassa had been home safe and sound for months, he was still plagued by an unreasonable fear of losing her again . . . and a total unwillingness to share her with anyone else.

"Dan, please . . ." Cassa pleaded, seeing the wildness

deep in his eyes. "Gir is a friend," she finished softly.

"I know. But *I* want to buy your clothes." He fought to suppress his possessiveness.

Confused emotion swept over Cassa and her eyes filled with tears. Immediately contrite, Dan grasped her forearms in an iron grip, and cried, "Darling, I didn't mean to upset you. Forgive me. I'm a stupid fool. Keep the clothes . . . as a gift from Gir." He muttered the last words into her hair.

"He would be hurt if I didn't," she tried to explain. "He really did get them at rock-bottom prices, and they're so lovely." She spoke from the safety of his chest. "And, Dan, I'm crying because my hormones are out of kilter, not—"

"Trying to spare my feelings, love?" Dan interrupted, cradling her to him, his lips moving over her hair and down to her cheekbones.

"Not at all. I'm just telling you the truth."

"Fine," he soothed, damning himself for being twelve kinds of a fool for upsetting her. "Let's forget we even had this conversation, darling."

"But Dan . . ."

Dan was shushing her as Dendor poked his head into the back room. "Dan, the car is here to take you to the airport. Ah, Cassa child, how pretty you look."

"Doesn't she?" Dan admired her, then kissed her again. "I'll be back as early as I can tomorrow."

Cassa had dinner with Len and Maddy that night, and later in the week, when Dan was home, she returned the favor at Cornhill.

Cassa would have been thoroughly happy, but the feeling that Dan had some secret reservations about becoming a father was never far from her consciousness. The issue cast a pale shadow on their life together. She wanted to talk to him about it, yet she was reluctant to hear him confirm her unspoken suspicion: that he would have preferred to remain childless.

One evening, just as they were leaving Len and Maddy's, Dan chuckled. "Sometimes I think Len is more excited about this baby than we are."

"I'm excited; though I obviously can't speak for you," Cassa said angrily.

He shifted gears and headed toward Main Street. "What are you saying, Cassa?" he asked warily.

Anger melted her long-held restraint, and the truth poured out of her. "Sometimes you act as though I were giving birth to a Minotaur, not a child." Her throat tightened; her eyes stung.

"Cassa, I want your baby."

"Our baby . . . *our* baby!" Cassa cried.

"Our baby," Dan amended. "Darling, I'm sorry if I don't seem enthusiastic, but I've been busy at work, running back and forth." He braked at an intersection.

"It's more than that. I can feel it."

He turned down Atkinson Street and pulled into their drive. After parking the car in the garage, they walked across their small yard into the utility room and through to the kitchen.

Dan took hold of her arm and forced her to face him. "Cassa, listen to me. I want the baby, and I'm going to love it. I'll be the kind of father you want me to be." His voice softened, became earnest, intense. "I promise you."

But she didn't want him to love their child for *her* sake. She wanted him to love the child for its own sake. But her mouth closed, and she nodded leaning against his chest. "All right, Dan."

"You look exhausted," he whispered, his hand smoothing her satiny black hair.

She nodded. Heartsick is what I am, Dan, she thought. But she said no more.

They went up stairs side by side, to their room. Dan helped Cassa with her zipper, then left her to shower. A half hour later Cassa stood in their room and gazed at her nude body in the full-length mirror—at the reddened stretch marks on her abdomen that nearly drove her crazy with itching. Not all the cocoa butter Dan slathered on her skin seemed to help for long. "Damn ugly tank," she muttered, turning this way and that.

"Wow!" Dan emerged from the bathroom, still drying

his hair with a towel. Eyes blazing, he declared, "If you're trying to seduce me, you're succeeding very nicely, my dear."

"Dan, how can you still want me when I look like the Little Red Engine That Could," Cassa wailed.

He shouted with laughter. "Darling, you're wonderful. Even more lovely than when we first met." He leaned down to touch the corner of her mouth with the tip of his tongue. "Shall I give you a back rub, then put some cocoa butter on your tum tum?"

"Tum tum?" Cassa smiled. "You sound like someone talking to a baby."

"I am. *You're* my baby." He put an arm around her, swung her onto the bed, and turned her on her side.

"I can't even sleep on my stomach anymore," Cassa grumbled, as Dan caressed her skin with cooling alcohol and then his warm hands.

"In a few months you'll be able to," he crooned as he pressed and massaged her aching back, moving his strong yet gentle hands down her buttocks to her thighs, calves, and ankles. "Feel better?"

"Uh huh."

"You know I love you, don't you, darling?"

She nodded with her cheek still pressed into the pillow.

"Have I told you I find it most erotic to make love to a pregnant lady? Especially a lady with such a delicious curve to her tum tum."

"Tum tum again." Cassa's eyes fluttered open. "You can't mean that—about finding me sexy when I look like a balloon."

"Oh, but I do. Your skin is like satin. Your breasts are so very full, my sweet, and they taste so good. Your eyes are like lustrous pearls, and when I touch you, you quiver. You're even sexier now that you're expecting, angel."

"I feel sexier," Cassa admitted. "Sometimes when we're working, I fantasize that you're making love to me."

"Lord, darling, don't ever tell me when you're having one of your fantasies. I would probably chase the customers away and order Dendor home. Don't tell me, please. We'd be out of business in six months."

Cassa laughed helplessly, turning over on her back, seeing the smile leave his eyes as they began devouring her body like a blue fire. How delightful! she mused. We're going to make love.

"What are you thinking? Your eyes are so hazy and slumbrous."

"I was thinking of this." She let her fingers pluck at the hair curling on his chest. "And this . . ." She slid lower, her hand capturing his manhood with a light-as-air caress, then gently rubbing his inner thighs.

"You think lovely things, angel," Dan murmured, his body crouched tentlike above, but not touching, hers.

"Don't I, though?" She gave a throaty chuckle as he arched his back and groaned. Her fingers continued seeking, and destroying what remained of Dan's restraint.

"Vixen," he muttered, sinking down beside her on the bed, his hands beginning a quest of their own. His were softer, more patient, more tender than hers had been, but soon the increasing urgency of his movements telegraphed his rising desire.

Cassa wriggled with joy as he slid up and down her body, his open mouth making her ache with swirling delight. "Nola told me I needed to exercise. I told her this was my favorite method," she teased.

Dan rose from her, his eyes glittering as he looked down at her. "Did you now?" he asked skeptically.

"No," she trilled. "But if I had, it would have been the truth." She pulled his head down and fitted her mouth to his. Their tongues dueled with sweet agony.

As usual Dan's tender entry into her body took her breath away. Passion overwhelmed her, and she writhed against him, moaning words of love.

"Easy, my angel. Let me do the work."

"Bossy," Cassa accused huskily, a familiar feeling that was both lassitude and tension building inside her. Her head moved restlessly on the pillow as Dan strived to bring her to fulfillment. They crested together like a rocket thrusting into the firmament, passing the moon and sun and shooting toward the farthest star.

"Dan," Cassa mumbled much later. She turned in his

arms and kissed his throat, burying all her fears under the knowledge that he loved her and she loved him.

The next day Dan brought the usual cup of weak lemony tea and soda crackers on a tray to their bedroom.

"I told you I don't have morning sickness anymore." Cassa smiled up at him as he plumped her pillows and placed the tray across her knees.

"You also told me how much better you feel after you've had the tea and crackers." He pointed to a small glass of apple juice that was also on the tray and four capsules. "Juice and vitamins for mama too." He sat down on the bed. "I have a surprise that—" His words were interrupted by a loud clatter on the stairs. Suddenly the bedroom door crashed open, and Nappy appeared in the doorway, panting and wagging his tail.

"Bad dog!" Mrs. Bills's voice came from downstairs. "You get back here right now."

Dan rose from the bed. "Fool. Stop laughing, Cassa. You're just encouraging him." Dan went into the hall and called down to the housekeeper. "We have Nappy up here with us, Mrs. Bills. I'll bring him down when I return with Cassa's tray."

"Thank you, Mr. Dan. Pesty creature . . ." Mrs. Bills's mutters faded away.

"Have you been annoying Mrs. Bills again, you naughty boy?" Cassa demanded of the dog, trying to look stern. But when Nappy cocked his head and wagged his tail, she laughed again.

Interpreting her response as a sign of acceptance, he bounded forward to the side of the bed, but then he came to a standstill and stared up at her expectantly. Nappy had been part of the Welles household long enough to know that if he jumped on the bed anywhere near Cassa, Dan would roar like all the banshees of Ireland. But the real punishment was being chained in the yard and not allowed inside for the rest of the day.

"Sweet boy, nice boy," Cassa crooned, reaching out to pat his head and fend him off at the same time.

After she'd finished eating and Dan had left with the dog, Cassa got out of bed, standing still for a moment to let her sudden vertigo subside before she headed for the shower. She'd just finished soaping herself under the warm water when she felt a sudden draft. She smiled as the shower door opened. She knew who it was.

"What are you thinking, standing there with your eyes squeezed shut, shampoo like a fluffy cap in your hair, tiny bubbles all over your body . . . here and here." Dan's voice took on a sensual slur.

"Aaagh! That shampoo tastes awful. Dan, you were saying something about a surprise for me when Nappy so rudely interrupted. What is it?"

"Get washed, my blossoming temptress, and I'll tell you," he teased her.

"Dan . . ." Cassa wailed, but he was already leaving the room, a sly smile on his face.

Cassa returned to the bedroom swathed in a bathsheet with a smaller towel twisted like a turban around her head. "Here I am. What's the surprise?"

"That's the shortest shower you've ever taken," he accused her with a grin.

"I'd rather have taken a bath, but I can't even get in the hot tub anymore unless you're there to pull me out," she complained.

"See how much you need me?" Dan began drying her body with quick love pats.

"Tell me the surprise."

"Okay." He settled her on his lap. "There's going to be an estate sale on East Avenue—one of those mansions you love—and I'm taking you there. Dendor thinks there'll be several nice orientals." His eyes glinted happily when she gasped with delight. "And Dendor insisted I take you because your eye for quality and color is second to none."

"Did he really say that?" Dan chortled as Cassa preened at his flattery.

"Pregnancy has made you vain," Dan pronounced, patting her on the backside, then going to the mirror to straighten his tie. "Just because you can lure me into bed with the wink of an eye, you think you're one special lady." He glanced at her in the mirror, his eyes lingering over her breasts. "And you are."

"Am I?" Cassa loved it when he said sweet things to her, even though she knew she looked like a blimp.

"Yes, angel, you are. Now get dressed. And wear that shiny silver suit I like."

"I can't wear that in the daytime. Silver satin is for evening, silly. How about the teal-blue silk tunic you like?"

Dan shrugged. "All right. But tonight I'm taking you out for dinner in that silver number. I love it when we dance and I get to slide against you."

"Daniel Casemore Welles!" Cassa laughed at him, then went to get dressed.

The drive across the river and up the wide, tree-lined East Avenue pleased Cassa. The thoroughfare was dotted with stone and brick mansions with sweeping green lawns. The styles ranged from colonial to Victorian, from Georgian to modern—a beautiful collection of homes.

Finally they turned into a half-moon driveway leading up to a gray stone house with an orange slate roof, and parked among cars behind a string of prospective buyers. Word of the sale had apparently spread.

Dan and Cassa stood looking up at the magnificent structure. "It's really a grand old place," he said, "but it must be impossible to heat. Still, I wish it were ours."

"We'd get lost in it." She glanced behind the house and exclaimed, "Look! The garage alone is three stories high. It's bigger than our entire house."

Dan held open the front door—a thick slab of oak set into a pointed arch in the Gothic manner. The large, circular foyer featured beautiful marble floors and a glittering crystal chandelier. A graceful staircase rose to a wide landing before dividing into two sections that led to the second floor.

"The inspection begins in the library," a youngish woman in a dark suit informed them, her eyes lingering on Dan.

"Thank you," Cassa said stiffly, giving her an icy glance.

As they moved away, Dan whispered, "What was that all about? You were a bit rude to that woman. It's not like you."

"I think it was rude of her to look at my husband with such obvious interest. He isn't available."

"I love it when you show your baser emotions," Dan

said with a smile as they entered the book-lined library.

Cassa felt herself being whisked away into a dream world. "Dan!" she hissed urgently, pulling on his coat sleeve. "A round Bokara! Look at the deep blue and turquoise!"

Dan lifted the tag and whistled softly. "They want a good price for it."

"Make them an offer," she begged.

He chucked her under the chin, nodded to an attendant, then shepherded her into another room.

Cassa glanced at the other items for sale, but the Bokhara was all she wanted.

Dan left her for a moment, returing a few minutes later. "You are now the proud owner of the Bokhara, my darling."

Cassa gave her husband a teary smile and a fierce hug.

9

AUTUMN SOON BECAME winter.

Snow covered the ground at Christmas and accumulated during January. But not all Cassa's urgings that Dan should go skiing with his friends, which he loved to do, could budge him from her side.

Cassa felt fine as she entered the final stage of her pregnancy. She continued to work at the store, but gave up handling customers and concentrated on keeping the books.

Sometimes on diamond-clear evenings she and Dan would go for short walks, admiring the crystal wonder of snow and ice on the neighborhood homes, the pink brick sparkling like pale rubies under the streetlights.

"I love winter," Cassa said, breathing in deeply as she waddled up the porch steps, Dan holding her tightly. "Of course, other winters I haven't looked like the snow plow." She sighed as they stepped through the front door.

"You're beautiful to me," Dan helped remove her coat, scarf, gloves, hat, and two extra sweaters, then settled her in a chair. "And I love our baby." He pulled off one of her boots and kissed her stomach, feeling a sting of tears even as he said the words. He *did* want this baby. He wanted to be its father more than anything in the world. But the black fear of losing Cassa kept enveloping him, no matter how often her doctor assured him she was perfectly healthy.

She sighed, rubbing her back, and said, "I think Nola is wrong about this being one baby," she said. "I must be having at least four . . . or five." She bit her lip as she saw the now familiar expression of worry pass over Dan's face. "Just kidding, love, truly I am. I'm very fit."

On February fourth Nola Jacobsen announced that the baby was positioning itself nicely, and predicted that Cassa would begin labor in another week or two.

That night, after Dan had turned Cassa for the tenth time and then fallen back to sleep, she lay staring at the ceiling, the twinges of pain in her lower back increasing. "Baby, you want to be born tonight, I think. Aaah," she moaned softly into the comforter that was pressed against her mouth.

"Honey," Dan mumbled from his cocoon of sleep. "Do you want to be turned over again?"

"No, I'm fine," she said calmly. There was no need to arouse him so soon.

"That's good." And Dan fell right back to sleep.

Two hours later Cassa managed to slide out of bed, but her water broke before she reached the bathroom. A strong contraction made her double over. "Dan!" she called.

"What?—Cassa, darling, where are you?"

"Almost to the bathroom. Dan, our child wants to be born." She heard a thud in the dark as his feet hit the floor, and then the bedside lamp flashed on and he was at her side.

He assessed the situation in an instant, scooped her up in his arms, and carried her back in bed. Cassa began breathing through her mouth and panting just as she'd been taught to do in the childbirth classes she and Dan had attended. Meanwhile, Dan phoned Nola, not taking his eyes off his wife, his own body breaking out in a cold sweat as he watched her body tighten with another contraction. "Yes, get the doctor and tell her to come quickly," he barked into the phone. "I'm taking my wife to the hospital now."

Bundling Cassa up like a refugee, he half carried, half led her to the car. "You're going to be just fine, my darling," he assured her, kissing the palm of one mittened hand when she groaned. He let loose a steady—but silent—stream of curses as the car crept slowly down the icy roads.

On the radio, the announcer urged motorists to proceed with extreme caution.

"Dan, it's getting harder to breathe. The pains—" Cassa gasped as another spasm rocked her.

"Hold on, darling. I can't help you and drive the car at the same time." Dan's voice was shaking.

"You may have to." Cassa panted as a feeling of tremendous pressure increased in her lower body. After what seemed like hours, Dan skidded to a stop in front of the well-lit emergency entrance, leaving the motor running as he came around to help her out of the car.

Two attendants in white coats appeared with a stretcher. "We'll take her, sir. You can go park the car," one said.

"*You* park my car," Dan ordered. "I'll take my wife. Just tell me where to go."

Nola met them at the entrance to the obstetrical unit. After taking one look at them, she rushed to Cassa's side.

Cassa screamed. "Dan!"

"My God, darling!"

In moments he was masked and gowned. His eyes never left Cassa's pain-wracked body as she was wheeled into the unit. Nola took charge, giving orders calmly but with complete authority. Dan murmured soothing words to Cassa and held her hand, leaning down to kiss and wipe her forehead as she sweated and strained to bring her child into the world.

It was a boy. Nola held the baby up to Cassa. "Well, Dan, what do you think?" his wife asked tremulously.

"Darling, thank God it's over and you're all right," he said, with barely a look at the infant.

"Dan, Dan." Cassa's voice cracked, her physical suffering no match for her mental agony. "Look at him—he has black hair. Listen to him howl, Dan."

"Yes, yes, my love. I see," he whispered, propping her up so she could watch the nurses washing the baby.

Soon Cassa slept. She half woke a few hours later and

sleepily told a nurse that she and her husband had decided to name the baby Daniel Casemore Welles, Jr.

She woke again much later, feeling alert but sore and stiff. Dan was there, along with a nurse and the baby. Cassa held her infant son and urged him to suck at her breast. Then the nurse—Miss Waite—took the baby from her.

Cassa slept intermittently for the rest of the day, and even though she'd protested that a private room was too expensive, she was secretly glad Dan had insisted on it. This way he could stay with her much longer.

They were holding hands that evening when Maddy came in, followed by Len and Gir.

"Maddy got the room number, and Len and I snuck up the stairs," Gir informed Cassa. "So, let's see this wonder of wonders."

Cassa unwrapped the blankets from the baby, who slept quietly beside her. Maddy sighed. "He's beautiful." Len's eyes were suspiciously moist as he agreed.

"He's red, wrinkled, and has a permanent frown," Gir stated flatly. "You should give him back."

"I'll give *you* back," Cassa fumed, cuddling her precious package.

Gir ducked behind Dan in mock terror.

"Dan, stop laughing," Cassa ordered huffily. "How can you allow that cretin to remain here?"

Dan lifted her hand to his mouth and nibbled on the end of her finger. "The baby *is* a bit wrinkled, love."

"I think he's perfect," Cassa declared, glaring from her husband to her fastidious friend.

"Then you're blind, Cassa, my love," Gir broke in. "He looks like an oversized apricot that was left in the sun too long." Ignoring the women's gasps, he added, "But since he'll be my godchild, I shall take him in hand immediately. He's bound to improve under my tutelage."

Maddy was restrained from throwing the water jug at her partner by a chuckling Len.

When Cassa referred to the baby as Dan C., Gir was outraged. "Dan C!" he said scathingly. "What a perfectly horrid name. Why don't you call him Case, or something like that."

Although it irked Cassa to do so, she had to admit the name had appeal. "Dan?"

He nodded. "It might save him from being known as Junior."

When Nurse Waite came to collect her charge, she frowned sternly at the group clustered around Cassa's bed. But when Maddy pleaded with her to let them stay just a few minutes longer, she nodded indulgently. "But I don't want you to stay long. This baby was born just a few hours ago, and his mother is tired."

"I feel wonderful," Cassa announced with a winsome smile, looking wistfully at the baby. "When will you bring him back to me?"

"When you've had a chance to rest." The nurse glared at them all, and hurried away, the swaddled bundle held safe in her arms.

Maddy sighed and leaned her head on her husband's chest. "He's one gorgeous baby, Cass."

"I know," Cassa said complacently, her eyes on Dan. "His father deserves some credit too." It startled her to see Dan's mouth tighten. "Darling, do you have a headache? Perhaps you should go home and lie down for a while. You hardly slept at all last night."

Gir studied Dan. "You do look done in, my good man. Come out for a drink with me. Maddy and Len can visit with Cassa."

"Another dictate from the gods," Len remarked with amused irritation. "Come along, my sweet. Cass looks ready for another nap. Why don't we stop for a nightcap—without your partner!"

"Oh, sweet blessings." Maddy closed her eyes in rapture.

Gir looked down his nose at them. "Plebeians." He kissed Cassa on the cheek. "Really, I suppose on a scale of one to ten, I could give your child a four—perhaps five, sweet Cassa."

"How would you like a black eye?" Cassa asked in dulcet tones.

Gir sighed. "I'll meet you downstairs, Dan. Try to control Dracula's mother, will you?"

"Are you calling the baby a monster?" Maddy cried,

lashing out at Gir as her husband held her around the waist. "I'm going to bust him in the chops."

"Really!" Gir said haughtily, and sailed out the room.

"I'm going to put out a contract on him," Cassa said, covering a yawn with her hand.

"I'll help." Maddy offered, kissing her cheek and promising to return before work the next morning.

Len kissed Cassa good-bye too, and they were gone.

"It's time this mama was asleep." Dan leaned over her, his expression intent. "How am I going to sleep tonight without you in my bed?" he mumbled into her hair, rubbing his face back and forth in its softness.

"I'll be home tomorrow," she promised, loving the feel of his hand kneading her sore stomach. "I still have a little basketball there," she said, grimacing.

"Give it time, woman. You just had a baby." Dan's hands trembled as he clutched her to him.

"Dan? Dan, what's wrong?" Cassa tried to look into his face, but he was holding her too tightly.

"Nothing. Nothing's wrong, my angel. I guess I do need to go home and take a nap. I'll be back as soon as I can."

"I know that." Cassa rubbed the stubble on his chin. "You look like a new rock star with that beard."

"Darling, I didn't scratch you, did I?"

"No." They kissed good-bye, and Cassa watched him stroll from the room, his slender, well-muscled body moving with athletic grace.

She bit her lip and considered her uneasiness once again. Dan wasn't really happy about the baby. He was trying, but he couldn't quite mask his true feelings. Cassa was certain no one else could sense the vibrations she'd detected from him, but she was sure they were there.

Sleep came like a soft cloud, enveloping her and wiping away all her worries, erasing all thought from her mind.

The next afternoon Daniel Casemore Welles went home with his parents, sleeping and dry, carefully bundled against the February cold.

Dan looked over at Cassa and the baby, and smiled. "It was hell sleeping without you last night. I finall had to hug the pillow and pretend it was you."

Cassa blinked, nodding. "I took the sleeping pill prescribed for me. We're awful fools, aren't we?"

"Awful." Dan lifted a corner of the blanket and peeked at the baby. "And how is the little guy today?"

"Your son is just fine," Cassa said in a soft voice.

Dan nodded, his lips pressed tightly together as he put the car in gear and drove out of the hospital parking lot. Cassa looked up at the stone-and-brick building, amazed that she had entered it to deliver her child less than two full days ago. She felt as though she had already been a mother for weeks. She sighed with well-being.

"Tired, darling?" Dan reached over to raise the heat in the car.

"No. Just feeling very good and very smug." She chuckled.

"You've conquered the world, have you?" Dan smiled as he drove carefully over the Clarissa Street Bridge. "The nurse I've hired will surprise you, I think."

Cassa was surprised. "You've hired her already? I thought you wanted me to check her out first."

"You have, my love, and you were very pleased with the way she handled Case," Dan answered.

"Dan, I never interviewed anyone for the job." Cassa grew flustered at the thought of facing a grim-faced woman who would want to monopolize her child, who wouldn't understand his already complex personality. We'll see just how long she stays around if I don't like the way she's handling Case, Cassa fumed to herself. Dan might be the father, but clearly he didn't understand these things.

"Stop looking so worried, my love." Dan parked the car and came around to open her door and lift the baby into the crook of his arm. He helped Cassa from the car and closed the door with his foot.

They hurried into the house, Dan cushioning the baby from the winter wind with his body. As they stood in the front foyer, Mrs. Bills hurried out of the kitchen, her face wreathed in smiles, another woman following at her heels.

"Nurse Waite!" Cassa was stunned. "I looked for you this morning to say good-bye." She glanced at her smiling husband, then back at the nurse, who reached for the baby and efficiently divested him of his outer wrappings.

"That's my surprise," Dan explained. "When I asked Nurse Waite about hiring a nurse, she told me she was just filling in at the hospital until one of the staff nurses returned from sick leave. Yesterday was her last day. After hearing you extol her virtues, and then looking at her resume, I hired her on the spot."

"You're wonderful." Cassa let Dan take her coat, then help her to a chair in the lounge.

Mrs. Bills stopped cooing over the baby just long enough to get the antique tea cart that had belonged to Uncle Aram. The spirit lamp had been lit under the silver coffeepot, and tiny home-baked French pastries were arranged on a silver platter.

"I feel as though I've just arrived with the Welles dauphin." Cassa chuckled, letting Dan put her feet on an antique needlepointed stool.

"And so you have," Mrs. Bills said staunchly, her gaze going to the sleepy infant cradled in the nurse's arms.

"Would you like to hold him, Mrs. Bills?" Cassa asked.

"Oh yes." She held out eager arms to Nurse Waite, who hesitated only slightly before handing him over. "He's so beautiful," the housekeeper murmured as Case opened hazy blue eyes to peer solemnly up at her.

Immediately Case's little mouth began to search blindly, making loud sucking noises. When his life sustenance wasn't forthcoming, he screwed up his face and howled.

Mrs. Bills beamed. "A good yell means a strong baby," she announced.

"Then he must be the strongest in town," Dan drawled.

"Give him to me." Nurse Waite lifted the squalling infant. "I'll change his diaper and bring him right back to you," she assured an anxious Cassa. Mrs. Bills bustled out to get fresh coffee.

"Darling . . ." Dan leaned over his wife and planted a kiss on her brow. "I think I'll go to the store for a while."

"Ducking out on all the noise and confusion?" Cassa ran the palm of her hand down his cheek.

"What else?" His mouth trailed down her face. "See you tonight, my love. I look forward to sleeping with you—

even if it is only sleeping we'll be doing," he said with a grimace, gave her a quick good-bye kiss, and left the room.

She gazed after him with a puzzled frown. When are you going to tell me what's bothering you, Daniel Casemore Welles? she mused. Will you ever tell me why it is you resent our son?

The next three weeks flew by for Cassa. People dropped in almost daily to see the baby, many of them neighbors from the Cornhill area.

Dendor arrived with gifts fit for a king. One was an heirloom oriental rug that had been in his family for over a hundred years. "I insist that this be put in his nursery and walked on so that it will not lose its natural sheen."

"Please, Dendor, let us put it on the wall," Cassa urged.

"All right. But my ancestor the camel driver, who crossed the Himalayan Mountains with rugs, will not appreciate it." Dendor started to frown, but his face lit up when he looked down at the baby. "He is very like his father and mother, I think."

"Yes." Cassa laughed, smoothing her son's silky cap of black hair. "We agree, don't we, Dan?"

"Yes," he answered, but he swallowed his wine in a single gulp and averted his eyes from her.

Cassa's mood changed abruptly. She could have sworn he'd been more accepting of the baby in the last week, but now . . . She simply couldn't figure him out.

One evening several weeks later they were sitting at the dinner table, the baby in a portable crib next to them. Dendor was their only guest.

"And, of course, here is good sound stock for him—Eastman Kodak, Xerox, Bausch and Lomb—so that you can begin his portfolio," Dendor explained.

"With nothing but Rochester companies in the portfolio, of course." Dan poured himself more wine, refusing Mrs. Bills when she offered him another portion of fresh sole stuffed with shrimp and vegetables. His grin was indulgent as he regarded the older man.

"Of course." Dendor shook his index finger. "The man is a fool who doesn't support his own community companies." He grinned. "But the man also is a fool who doesn't protect his rear. Included in the portfolio are IBM and A T and T."

Cassa and Dan laughed, then fell quiet as their friend brought a jewel case out of his pocket. "Perhaps someday this will belong to the wife of little Case, or"—he smiled at them—"perhaps to his sister."

"Not until he's sleeping through the night," Dan said with a groan.

"In the meantime, Cassa my child, this jewelry, which belonged to my wife, now belongs to you." Dendor slid the case toward Cassa.

"But Dendor," she began.

"No buts." He held up his hand.

Cassa opened the worn case and gasped at the necklace of luminous pearls with matching earrings and ring. "How beautiful," she said softly.

"Yes, they are—and real pearls they are, not cultured." Dendor nodded twice. "Now. Push the silver button there . . ."

Cassa pressed the tiny button and a slim drawer slid out of the bottom of the case. Inside were two rings—one a sapphire, one opal—and a pair of diamond clips. "It's too much," she protested, but she was forestalled by another raised hand. "Thank you, dear Dendor." She rose from her chair and gave him a big hug and a kiss. "I will be proud and happy to wear them."

"Then you honor me, child, and my beloved wife, Miriam."

After Dendor left that evening, Dan and Cassa sat in the living room admiring the jewelry. Cassa tried some of the pieces on for Dan.

"Ah, the perfect outfit for seduction—a string of pearls and nothing else." Dan growled and snapped his teeth as if to eat her up.

"Dan," Cassa murmured from the haven of his arms.

"Yes, my love?" His breath teased her hair as his hands roamed over her. It had been several weeks since they'd made love, and the deprivation had been hard on them both.

"Dan, would you like to have a baby—I mean another baby—right away?" Cassa asked, twisting his shirt button.

He drew back to look at her. "If you want another baby right away, fine—as long as the doctor says it's okay. Why do you ask?"

"I. . . I don't know." Cassa wanted to tell him how she felt, that she was sure he resented Case, but she couldn't bring herself to give voice to her fears. "I thought a playmate might be good for Case."

"Fine. After you've had a good checkup from Nola and she gives us the go-ahead, we can start trying. How's that?"

"Good." Cassa leaned up to kiss the corner of his mouth.

Dan stiffened. "Cassa, my darling, please . . ."

"By the way, did I tell you I went to see Nola today? One of the things she told me was that I could resume having relations with my husband—if he's willing, of course," Cassa teased.

Dan's eyes sparkled down at her. "Heaven forbid that you would force me to make love to you." His mouth moved across her cheek as his fingers fumbled at the buttons on her blouse. "For weeks I've been watching Case suckle at your breast, going slowly insane. I have a need for your sustenance myself. Thank God, Mrs. Waite insisted that he go into his nursery now—right next to her room." Dan leered at his wife.

"Mr. Welles, have you got designs on my body?" Cassa said with mock indignation. Her body was already shuddering with yearning for him.

"Designs, plans, you name it." Dan's words were slurred against her breast. "Can I talk you into coming upstairs to see my etchings?"

"Do you consider me an art critic?"

"Uh-huh." Her husband groaned thickly, his tenuous control slipping.

"Wonderful. That makes it so much easier. I was happy it wouldn't be too hard to convince you to—eeeee! Dan, that feels wonderful."

"*You* feel wonderful." He leaned down and lifted her into his arms. "Oh, Cassa, I've been waiting to do that for ages."

"But I was too heavy for you, is that it?" She chuckled into his neck.

"No, you weren't too heavy—not that you weren't quite a handful. Ouch, you're biting my neck!" Dan grinned and carried her into the foyer. "When you were pregnant I was so afraid of hurting you in any way that I didn't dare carry you."

"You fool," Cassa crooned as they reached the upper hall and entered their bedroom.

"Darling, you wouldn't like to pander to one of my fantasies, would you?" Dan let her slide down his body, his eyes frankly enjoying the sight of her full breasts in the lacy bra. "Lord . . . you are so lovely. How do you manage to get more beautiful every day?"

"Taking buttermilk baths?"

"Do you do that?" His eyes darkened to midnight blue.

"No, but I think that's what you're supposed to do to stay beautiful," Cassa babbled, not concentrating on the words she was saying, only aware of the wonder of Dan's Dan's body as she helped him undress.

"Let's buy several gallons of buttermilk. The thought of you in such a bath . . ." He pulled her tight against him. "See what you do to me, sexy lady?"

"Ummm, it feels nice. I've missed this." Her eyes closed as she leaned against him, and he removed the rest of her clothes.

"Missed it? I damn near died wanting you."

"What were you saying about indulging one of your fantasies?"

He leaned back from her, his eyes roving up and down her nude body. "Would you mind coming to bed wearing just those pearls that Dendor gave you?"

Cassa could feel her blood coursing through her veins. "That sounds fantastic." She whirled away to reach for the jewel case on her dresser. Then, wagging her finger at him, she skipped into the dressing room.

"Wait," Dan called to her. "I don't want you to leave me. Forget the pearls and come out here."

Cassa ignored him. Her eyes swept the bottom of the closet in search of the pale pink satin slippers with the four-inch heels that Dan had once bought her as a joke. "Watch out, Mr. Welles," she called. "Here comes Mrs. Welles, your femme fatale." She laughed softly as she removed her earrings, brushed out her hair, then donned the pearls and slippers. She regarded herself in the full-length mirror, grimacing at her round tummy but otherwise pleased with the effect. She dabbed perfume on her ankles, behind her knees, on her elbows, and at the base of her throat, then opened the door.

Dan was sitting on the bed waiting for her. The only light came from a small lamp near him. Cassa walked across the room to her husband, stepping into the halo of light. "Here I am."

He didn't answer, but his gaze was smoldering, his body taut with restrained desire. He moved to rise, but Cassa held up her hand.

"No, I'm coming to you," she said softly. She sat down on the bed, and slid toward him, still wearing the satin shoes. "Do you like the fantasy so far?" she asked.

"It's definitely a collectors' item." Dan didn't try to clear the hoarseness from his throat.

"Are you a collector?"

"Yes."

"Then will you please collect me?" Cassa said breathlessly, leaning toward him.

"I'm so aroused I'm afraid I'll blow up if I touch you." His voice was just audible.

"Try," Cassa begged, rubbing her breasts against his chest and kissing his shoulder.

Dan closed his eyes. "I think there's such a thing as loving a person too much. I love you that way. You drive me wild, Cassa." His hand closed around her waist, and then with one speedy motion, she was in his lap, cradled against him. "Do I get to take off the slippers, or do we leave them on?"

"It's your fantasy," Cassa answered, nibbling his chin, then covering his face with tiny kisses. "I'm your lady of the evening . . . yours to command."

"Then why do I have the feeling I'm the slave?" Dan shifted his body so that Cassa could feel the hard thrust of him beneath her. "I love you, wife."

"I love you, husband." Cassa gulped, fast losing control

as Dan began caressing her body. All the sensitive areas that had missed his touch during the last couple of months seemed to take fire as he explored them with his tongue and hands.

He slid her body down onto the bed and placed himself beside her so they faced each other, eye to eye, nose to nose. "You are all of life to me, Cassa. Without you, I'm hollow, empty . . ."

Cassa nodded. "Me too." She stroked his cheek with a hand that trembled.

"It's a very well-kept secret how erotic married love can be." Dan groaned as he leaned down to rub his tongue around her navel. "You taste so good—sweet, but with a tang of salt. I love it."

"Salt isn't good for you," Cassa babbled, clutching him as his mouth traveled over her body, making her spine arch, sending colorful pinwheels and stars shooting behind her eyes, filling her limbs with tingling excitement at the thought of what was to come.

"I tried to make it good for you, my angel, but—"

"It is good. I love it," Cassa assured him, panting.

He let his hand slip down her body, his fingers tentative in their intimate search.

"Darling, this isn't the first time we've made love," Cassa teased him, her breath coming more and more quickly. She ached with desire for him.

"I know, but you've had a baby . . . and . . . and—" He took in a shaky breath.

Words tumbled out of Cassa's mouth as she hastened to assure him that she was happy, that she wanted him, that he was sunlight and moonbeams to her, that the stars dipped and swayed because he loved her. "Do it, Dan. Love me. I want you very much." The words sounded solemn in the silent room, but the lightning inside her brought a smile to her face. Happiness made her want to shout.

He eased his hips down on her as though she might break beneath him. When he felt her body close around him like a velvet glove, control left him and he pulled her closer, ever closer, as he initiated a rhythm that brought them into another realm. They merged with one another, body and soul, finding fulfillment in the ultimate union.

Cassa's breath was still coming rapidly when Dan cuddled her close to his body and murmured, "Sleep, my angel, sleep. I will need you all my life."

Cassa collapsed, smiling, and pressed her mouth to his chest. "This is such a lovely way to end the day... I'll be your lady of the evening anytime."

"How about my lady of the morning? How about noon? Brunch?"

"All of the above." Cassa yawned and snuggled against him. "'Night."

The next morning at five Case demanded his breakfast. Dan brought the baby into the bedroom, having changed his diaper and put on a clean stretchsuit. "Here's the heir." Dan still looked bleary-eyed as he settled the baby at Cassa's breast.

"Darling, you shouldn't have gotten him. Mrs. Waite can do that."

"Never." Dan yawned, leaning over Cassa to gaze at the baby. "Miss reveille? Me?" He stifled another yawn and plumped up Cassa's pillows. "Hi, tiger." Dan touched one of Case's tiny fists, which opened and curled around his finger. Dan stood motionless. "Do you see that, Cassa? Lord, he's strong." Dan inched over so that he could pull Cassa onto his chest without releasing the baby's grip on his finger. "He's getting bigger. I can see the difference."

"He has an appetite like a stevedore," Cassa whispered, ecstatic that Dan hadn't left the room, as he often did when she nursed the baby.

"I thought a baby's hair fell out and grew in another color after a while," Dan murmured, stroking Case's downy black hair.

"Some babies do, but our son is different."

"Are you saying he's special, Mama?" Dan kissed his wife on the corner of her mouth.

"He *is* special." Her voice was low. "He looks just like you."

Dan stiffened. His mouth twisted in a mockery of a smile. His eyes darted away. "Of course he's special, aren't you, tiger?" he said with false brightness.

Daniel Casemore Welles, Jr., slid from his mother's

breast, his tiny mouth open and damp, his eyes fluttering in serene satisfaction.

Cassa lifted the tiny body up and kissed his head. "Dan, would you hold him for me so I can go to the bathroom?"

Dan hesitated, his anxious eyes on the yawning baby. He nodded. "Don't be gone too long. If he sees me, he might cry."

"Don't be silly." Cassa laughed, sprinting for the bathroom, pleased by the sight of Case snuggling up against her husband. Dan had held the baby many times, but he never seemed to enjoy it. She had decided not to force the baby on him, but she took every opportunity to bring father and son into close contact.

She emerged from the bathroom a few minutes later, still in her robe, and paused in the doorway. Dan was cradling the baby to his chest and singing, "Hush, little baby, don't you cry," in a faint but clear voice. The baby was blinking up at his father, wide awake, his fists waving in the air, blowing bubbles from his mouth.

Dan looked up, his eyes shining. "Cassa, I think he just smiled at me. I mean it. All of a sudden it happened. I thought I was going to have a heart attack. He's brilliant!"

"Just like his daddy."

"Of course. Just like me." He glanced at his watch. Cassa thought she saw a flash of pain in Dan's eyes before he smiled. "Well, I guess I'd better take my shower," he said, glancing at his watch.

Suddenly the magic moment was gone, and Cassa didn't know why. She took the baby from Dan and checked to see if his diaper was dry. It wasn't. She went to the nursery to change him before joining Dan for breakfast.

While she was sipping orange juice and swallowing the vitamins that Dan had laid out on her plate, she tried to get him to speak about their child. "You do think he's beautiful, don't you?"

"Sure," Dan said, leaping to his feet. He came around the table to kiss her, mumbling something about being late for a meeting. As he hurried out the door, Cassa's heart sank.

10

IT WAS APRIL. The long winter was over. Slush the color of brown sugar still covered the streets and sidewalks, but yellow and purple crocuses were already peeping up in the Cornhill gardens. The days were cold but sunny. Soon it would be time to take Case, now two months old, out in his stroller.

Cassa was more deeply enthralled with her son each day, and she could see that Dan had finally begun to succumb to their child's obvious charms. At night when he came home from work he would kiss her, then rush to pull the baby from his playpen for a great big hug.

It was even more amusing to see how protective of the baby Nappy had become. Though he wasn't allowed too close to Case, the big Bouvier would lie nearby for hours, watch the child and wagging his tail contentedly. Matt the Cat also had to watch from afar, but he too was fascinated by the infant.

One afternoon Cassa was straightening the master bedroom when Dan phoned.

"What a sexy "hello" you have," Dan said with a growl. "I don't want you talking to other people in that voice."

"Hello, darling. How are things at the store?"

"Dendor says business is down because you're not here. I keep trying to convince him that I'm really prettier than you are."

"You are."

"Stop that," Dan said huskily. "I'm getting an embarrassing bulge in my clothes."

"Do come home. The remedy is waiting here for you," Cassa purred in her sultriest voice.

"Lord, they'll disconnect our phone. Honey, listen to me. No more hanky-panky on the phone. I have something to tell you, but I want you to find the nearest chair and sit down first."

Immediately Cassa's common-sense went out the window. Terrible visions flashed through her mind, the worst involving Dan's declaration that he was leaving her. Her ears thrummed; her eyes stung. She clutched the phone like a lifeline.

"Darling? Cassa?"

"I'm here . . . and I'm sitting down."

"I called the people in New York about the rug auction, and one of the owners of the firm suggested that we have the meeting in Bermuda, not New York. How would you like to spend six days at the Loew's Bermuda Beach? Of course, there'd be meetings every morning, but we'd have the afternoons and evenings free."

"You aren't leaving me?" Cassa let out a sigh of relief.

"What are you talking about? Are you all right? You sound funny." Dan's voice was harsh with concern.

"No, no, don't worry. I'm just acting crazy—postpartum blues or something. I . . . I . . . for a moment I thought you might be leaving me." She took in a shuddering breath.

"Angel, I'm coming home for lunch," Dan said firmly, his heartbeat accelerating. "I'm in the mood to prove a point or two."

"What about Mrs. Bills?" Cassa said.

"The hell with her. She can walk the baby while I infuse my wife with confidence."

"Naughty man," Cassa teased.

"Get your pearls on," Dan murmured before hanging up.

The days before they left for Bermuda were filled with Cassa's frantic packing and anxious instructions. Not all of Mrs. Bills's and Nurse Waite's placating assurances could quiet her fears upon leaving her baby for the first time. Still, she looked forward to being alone with Dan.

On the plane out of Boston's Logan Airport, where they'd caught the connecting flight to Bermuda, Dan placed a hand under hers, his fingers, strong and blunt, dwarfing her soft, delicate ones. "Your hand in mine. That's all I'll ever need for power, for strength," he said.

"Me, too," Cassa murmured. "Isn't it funny that we never went to Bermuda before? We've been to the Bahamas, Jamaica, Barbados, St. Thomas . . ."

As Cassa paused, trying to remember all the places they'd been together, she glanced out of the window at the breathtaking scene below. She gasped with delight at the clear turquoise waters and the coral reefs she could see stretched out for miles below as the plane banked and began its descent.

They stepped from the plane into balmy air, went through Customs and reclaimed their baggage quickly, and hailed a taxi in the glistening sunshine.

"It's so blue and white and clean," Cassa exclaimed as they crossed the causeway, passed a military installation, and took the curving road into the old capital of St. George.

"The houses look like French bonbons—pink and cream, white and blue—and that lovely turquoise color that's in our Kerman rug."

"That color is called Bermuda blue," the dark-skinned taxi driver said, his British accent sounding pleasant to Cassa's ears.

Their suite was large and spacious, with a sitting room, bedroom, and bath. There was also a balcony that overlooked the ocean. Cassa took a deep breath of pungent sea air and sighed when she felt Dan's arm go around her. "I'm going to like it here," she said.

"I'm going to like being with you here," he murmured.

Dan had to check in with the convention people and place his name on the auction list. Security would be high, so they'd need passes in order to enter the auction rooms where the expensive new and used rugs were being sold.

That evening they went into Hamilton to dine and dance. Though Cassa was surprised to learn that most of the "tropical" food she was eating was imported from the United States, it did not dampen her delight in the well-prepared meal or the beautiful surroundings. They listened to island music, then danced to American tunes from the thirties and forties.

"This is wonderful." Dan hummed along with the band as he and Cassa swayed to ballads of yesteryear, their arms tight around each other.

"Ummm." Cassa didn't even open her eyes.

"Ah, lady, I know we've just met, but would you sleep with me tonight? Not that you'll be sleeping," Dan said softly, his teeth nipping her neck.

"How dare you, sir!" Cassa sniffed indignantly. "By the way, what's your room number, you sexy man?"

"Never mind the number, just let me drag you there." As Dan gazed down at her, the amusement in his eyes turned to burning desire.

"Or I could drag you."

"The game's over, darling. See what I mean?" He pressed his lower body against her.

"Daniel Casemore Welles!" Cassa laughed at him. "And you the father of a baby boy." She sucked in a breath as she saw the flash of pain in his eyes before he turned quickly away. But then he was smiling again, comforting her, warming her, loving her.

They left the restaurant hand in hand. Dan called a taxi to take them back to their hotel.

In the cab, he held her close, whispering love words in her ear. Cassa wanted desperately to ask him about his feelings for their baby, but she hesitated to risk spoiling the warmth between them.

When they reached their rooms, Dan gave her no chance to speak. He enfolded her in his arms and began kissing and fondling her. With a fierceness born of deep frustration and an overwhelming need to communicate with him, Cassa gave him back kiss for kiss, embrace for embrace.

The heat of love flared relentlessly between them until the familiar ache of desire made Cassa moan out loud. "I love you, Dan."

"And I you, my darling." He lifted his head from the pearly skin of her breasts. "There are no words to describe my emotions, the undying love and passion I feel for you." His mouth moved up and down her body, and she moaned softly as his lips climbed the mountain of rapture. Their eyes wide open, they gazed adoringly at each other, as their writhing bodies expressed the driving need that was as old as man and as necessary as death.

But as Cassa sensually explored her husband's body, her son's face came vividly to mind, haunting her with the unanswered question: Why did Dan resent his son? Then she gasped as the heat and urgency of Dan's movements wiped away all thought and they gave themselves freely to one another.

But as they lay there afterward, their bodies damp, Cassa knew she could wait no longer to learn the truth of Dan's feelings for his son. No matter what the cost, what the pain, she had to know. And she had to know now.

She swung her feet to the floor and stood up, sliding her arms into her silk wraparound robe, facing away from Dan toward the balcony. Sheer lemon-colored curtains belled out in the soft breeze, muting the moonlight that filtered into the room.

"Cassa? What are you doing, darling?"

She could tell from the sound of Dan's voice that he was still lying in bed. When she heard the rustle of crisp sheets, she said, "No, stay there. I think I can say this better if I'm not looking at you." Cassa swallowed, trying to steady her voice.

"What is it you have to say, Cassa?" Dan asked carefully. She sensed his wariness, the mounting tension between them.

Determined to finally reveal the fears she'd hidden from him for so long, Cassa said, "I think you love our son, Dan. But something is wrong and I don't know what it is. I've watched you play with Case, laugh with him"—she made a sweeping gesture with her hand—"even feed and change him, but the feeling persists that something is wrong."

When she heard the sheets rustle again, she rushed on. "Please, stay there. I have to finish this." She drew a painful breath into her lungs. "I love you, Dan, and I want us to be a family, but I have to know what's wrong—and there *is* something wrong, so please don't say it's nothing. From the time I told you I was pregnant, I've sensed a reserve in you, a drawing back. At first I thought it was because you didn't want me to have a baby."

"No," Dan denied.

"Then I thought it was because my swollen body repelled you."

"Never."

"But you showed me so much love, I knew that couldn't be it. When Case was born, you were obviously concerned about me, but—"

"Cassa, please. We don't have to talk about this."

"Yes, we do," she cried, whirling toward the darkened bed, barely able to make out his silhouette as he sat there, poised as if preparing to bolt. "We do," she repeated more softly. "You hardly touched him when we first brought him home. It was as though you were struggling against loving your own son."

"I will always love anything or anyone that is yours," Dan said with conviction.

"Why do you talk in that evasive way?" Cassa demanded, her voice rising. "We're talking about our *son!*"

"Yes. And I love him, Cassa. I mean that. I didn't at first, but I do now." The words seemed forced from Dan's throat.

"Why didn't you love him at first? Why did it take so long?" Cassa's throat was tight with unshed tears.

"It didn't take long. He was home just a few days before I was totally hooked. He had me tight in that fat fist of his." Dan gave a choked laugh.

"But tell me why you fought loving your own son!"

"Cassa, don't. I couldn't forget how hurt you'd been—how lost." Dan's voice was filled with pain.

"What do you mean? Do you mean when I returned from

Suwanon?" Cassa spread her hands wide in puzzlement. "What does that have to do with our baby?"

"You told me how they . . . how they abused you . . . hurt you. When I looked at you pregnant, when I saw the baby, I remembered that. I couldn't get it out of my mind."

"Dan, I . . ." Cassa stared across the darkened room as Dan rose from the bed and came toward her, his arms outstretched, his nude body gleaming silver in the moonlight.

"I'll have nightmares for the rest of my life, I know that," he said, "but I can't wipe it from my mind. They hurt you," he snarled pulling her into his arms, his hands trembling as he tenderly caressed her, his whole being pushing away the image of the pain she had had to endure.

Cassa felt stunned, as though she had just been whirled through space. "Dan, listen to me."

"I'm listening." His breath stirred the fine hair at her temples. His arms closed viselike around her. No one would ever hurt her again, he vowed deep in his soul.

"Dan, about me in Suwanon . . ." Cassa took in a shuddering breath.

"Sweetheart, don't talk about it if it hurts you." Dan bent his body protectively over hers.

She looked up at him, her love shining in her eyes. But before she could speak, Dan swept her into his arms and carried her back to bed, mumbling about drafts from the window and the dangers of catching cold. He sat down in the middle of the bed with Cassa cradled in his lap.

"Darling," she said, lightly stroking his cheek. "Aren't you going to let me talk?"

He turned his face into her palm, his tongue pleasantly rough on her sensitive skin. "Talk, if you have to. But I don't know if I can stand to hear this. I don't *want* to know, Cassa."

She lay a gentle finger on his lips. "Shhh. We should have talked long ago," she said, shaking her head. "Why didn't I realize why you were suffering so? All this time I thought you resented Case."

Dan took a deep breath and nodded. "I did. But I had myself in check. I made up my mind to love the child because he was yours." He held her tighter for a moment.

"I had a few bad times—when you first told me you were pregnant; when I watched you in the delivery room, suffering so much."

"I'll have you know I had a very smooth, easy delivery." Cassa thumped his chest, all aglow at the thought of their future together.

"You were in pain," Dan said angrily.

"Daniel Casemore Welles, I have never known you to be so difficult." She put both hands over his lips. "Now, I'm going to tell you a story about a woman who became trapped in an explosion in an embassy." She soothed Dan again when he stiffened. "I don't remember much about my trip to the place where I was held, but the man at the State Department told me that, because the Suwanese thought I was a French national, they held me as a hostage for the release of their friends. There were four of us—one other woman, who had been on a fact-finding trip for the United Nations, and two men, one of whom was Marcel Cyr, a man I met at the Suwanese marketplace buying rugs. He invited me to the French consulate for dinner that night." She swallowed. "It was Marcel who urged me to assume the identity of Marie Dugault. Since we were in a land that had no treaty agreements with the United States, he thought my chances would be better if they assumed I was a French national." She shrugged and tried to smile. "A Mr. Lawrence of the State Department told Len and me that I made a mistake, that I would have been better off telling them the truth."

Dan groaned. "For nine months I thought you were dead. I'd wake up in the morning wondering why it felt as if I had a two-ton cement block on my chest. Then I'd remember..." He fell silent.

"But you had Carla!" The words were out before Cassa had fully formed them in her mind.

"Were you jealous?" Dan's smile was twisted.

"I could have killed you." Cassa sighed.

"That wouldn't have been hard to do. I was already more than half dead. I didn't care if I married her—or if I didn't, for that matter—although I think I still might have balked at the altar. The few times I came out of the black fog I was walking around in, I realized what a shark she was. I felt as though I was sinking in quicksand, a real-life nightmare. Nothing seemed real. It was all gray. I didn't want to do anything that would upset the gray numbness of my life. It might have brought back feeling again, and I knew I couldn't stand that. So I just let things ride."

"I know. I do understand. But it kills me to think of you even kissing that woman—kissing anyone but me."

"Then you imagine how I've been feeling every time I think of those men—"

"Dan, listen to me," Cassa broke in. "I was strip-searched—and a few times the female guard left the door open as a joke so the men could leer and make ribald remarks. But—and this is very important—we were almost always well treated. No one molested us. No man ever touched me."

Dan leaned over and turned on the lamp, his face white in the muted light. "Are you saying that no one ever raped you? That they didn't assault you?" His eyes bore into hers.

"No one has ever had sex with me but you," Cassa said softly. "I'm very happy that you were determined to love any child of mine and that you *did* love Case even though you thought he was a product of rape, but"—she grinned at him—"you are a very virile man. I became pregnant very soon after my return."

"Then no one raped you?" Dan repeated in awe. "Oh, darling, it really didn't matter to me about the baby. It was just that I couldn't stop imagining how it must have been for you. I wanted to kill them." His voice quavered. "When you seemed so happy about the baby you were carrying, I was shocked, but I made up my mind right away. The child would be ours." He took a deep breath. "Then I saw you go through the labor, and I hated the child—at first. But in a few short days I knew I loved him as much as you did."

"I love you, Daniel Casemore Welles. Not once did you say anything negative to me about the rape—yet I know it's not uncommon for a man to reject a woman who has been raped. It doesn't matter that I wasn't raped. What matters is that you were able to put it behind you and love me even more beautifully than before." She shushed him once more when he began to speak. "And I love you for another reason—for the way you've treated our son. You're a very special man."

"My lady, my lady," Dan groaned. "You are all the world to me, Cassa."

"If you don't make love to me right this minute, I don't know what I'll do."

"Say no more, angel." He eased her back on the bed, picked up one slender foot, kissing each toe, then moved on to the other foot and all the rest of her body, his tongue intruding into the core of her, making her cry out with joy.

As always their passion built to explosive proportions. But Cassa sensed a change in their lovemaking, a new freedom yet a deeper involvement. It was the purest yet most erotic togetherness they had ever shared.

Epilogue

THE FOLLOWING SPRING, during the annual Cornhill Festival, Cassa sat in her front yard with a very excited one-and-a-half-year-old Case and the new baby, Madeleine Louise—or May Lou as her big brother pronounced it.

Dan came out of the house in tennis shorts and a terry-cloth shirt, both of Bermuda blue, which his wife fondly insisted was the very color of his eyes. He kissed Cassa on the cheek and sat down on the ground between her chair and the baby's crib. Together they watched the crowds of people that strolled down Atkinson Street, stopping to check out the vast variety of crafts and snacks for sale, enjoying the music of several country and rock bands along the way.

Mrs. Bills emerged from the house with a tray bearing frosted glasses and a pitcher. "I don't trust the way they make their lemonade," she said, looking skeptically across the street at a stand with a huge cardboard lemon attached to it.

"Me," Case declared, standing on sturdy legs and toddling over to Mrs. Bills, who poured him some lemonade in a plastic cup.

"Why don't you and Mr. Dan walk around the festival, Miss Cassa?" Mrs. Bills suggested. "I'll watch the children. Come on, Case, I've brought your engine out for you." Mrs. Bills indicated a plastic fire engine that Case could propel with his feet.

Dan and Cassa watched their son for a moment, then glanced at their sleeping daughter before passing through the wrought-iron gate into the leisurely moving crowd.

"I thought I was happy when we first got married," Dan began, "but I know now that that happiness was just a foreshadowing of what we have now." He tucked Cassa's hand through his arm and gazed tenderly down at her.

They stopped at a booth displaying seascape oil paintings. Cassa pointed to one titled *Bermuda Adventure* in which high waves crashed over the side of a launch as the captain in a sou'wester struggled to keep his boat on keel. The turquoise water was just as she remembered it.

"We'll take it," Dan said, pointing to the painting. After he'd paid for it in cash, Dan and Cassa stood staring at their purchase while throngs of people moved around them.

"Now I know I'm home," Cassa said. When Dan looked at her inquiringly she explained, "When I came back from Suwanon, I felt such a sense of homecoming each time you held me. But in Bermuda when we cleared the air..."

"I know what you mean," Dan interjected. "The cobwebs were swept away. The last remaining barriers destroyed. Nothing stood between us but our love." He bent closer to her. "I love you, wife of mine. You will always be my homecoming."

DON'T MISS THESE TITLES IN THE SECOND CHANCE AT LOVE SERIES

MOONLIGHT RHAPSODY #190
by Kay Robbins

Years ago Lacy Hamilton left celebrated concert pianist Randall St. James; now he seeks to win her back. But Lacy knows that loving a legend means asking for heartbreak...

SPELLBOUND #191
by Kay Nevins

In lush Ireland poet Brian O'Bannon charms biologist Miranda Dunn with clever words and a blithe spirit. But she distrusts the mesmerizing spell he casts...

LOVE THY NEIGHBOR #192
by Frances Davies

Sophisticated department store vice-president Nell Carlton has an unerring eye for style but not for love—until her neighbor rough-and-ready newspaper editor S.F. Shea, storms into her life.

LADY WITH A PAST #193
by Elissa Curry

When theater veteran Elizabeth Bradford is trapped inside a stage prop with virile Lane Remington, her initial chagrin turns to throbbing awareness...

TOUCHED BY LIGHTNING #194
by Helen Carter

Quiet, elegant speech therapist Joanna Greer vowed never to give herself to another man. But tough and tender Cliff Duquesne shatters her good intentions...

NIGHT FLAME #195
by Sarah Crewe

As steel mill consultant to Mark Somers, the golden boy who once rejected her, Sharon Dysart is determined to exorcise her youthful infatuation. But their attraction smolders...intense, inexorable...

#69

HERE'S WHAT READERS ARE SAYING ABOUT

"Your TO HAVE AND TO HOLD series is a fabulous and long overdue idea."
*—A. D., Upper Darby, PA**

"I have been reading romance novels for over ten years and feel the TO HAVE AND TO HOLD series is the best I have read. It's exciting, sensitive, refreshing, well written. Many thanks for a series of books I can relate to."
*—O. K., Bensalem, PA**

"I enjoy your books tremendously."
*—J. C., Houston, TX**

"I love the books and read them over and over."
*—E. K., Warren, MI**

"You have another winner with the new TO HAVE AND TO HOLD series."
*—R. P., Lincoln Park, MI**

"I love the new series TO HAVE AND TO HOLD."
*—M. L., Cleveland, OH**

"I've never written a fan letter before, but TO HAVE AND TO HOLD is fantastic."
*—E. S., Narberth, PA**

***Name and address available upon request**